NEW GIRL IN CAMP

The Jeep drove into camp. Marissa could tell by the sunglasses that Sin was driving. Her heart jumped. He must have a free hour too!

"You like him, don't you?" said Alicia. They giggled like little girls and hopped off the fence to go toward Sin. Jamie got out of the back, and Dark with him.

"My goodness," said Alicia. "Charles must have closed down the boys' side. Look at all these terrific specimens of manhood descending on us."

Sin opened the passenger door.

Alicia and Marissa strolled toward the boys. We're being very obvious, thought Marissa, wishing she had more of a reason to rush the Jeep. She got nervous at the idea of the boys watching her approach.

But they were not watching her.

They had not even seen her.

Sitting in front, enjoying the adoration, was a girl. Afterward Marissa thought it amazing that she had characterized Cathy as "a girl." For Cathy was the most beautiful girl Marissa had ever seen in her life.

She was not so much blond as golden.

She was not so much beautiful as ethereal.

Sin didn't even see Marissa. . . .

Other Bantam Starfire Books you will enjoy

CAMP
GIRL-MEETS-BOY

___

CAROLINE B. COONEY

BANTAM BOOKS
NEW YORK · TORONTO · LONDON · SYDNEY · AUCKLAND

RL 6, IL age 10 and up

CAMP GIRL-MEETS-BOY
A Bantam Starfire Book / August 1988

The Starfire logo is a registered trademark of Bantam Books, a division of Bantam Doubleday Dell Publishing Group, Inc. Registered in U.S. Patent and Trademark Office and elsewhere.

ISBN 0-553-27273-X

Published simultaneously in the United States and Canada

Bantam Books are published by Bantam Books, a division of Bantam Doubleday Dell Publishing Group, Inc. Its trademark, consisting of the words "Bantam Books" and the portrayal of a rooster, is Registered in U.S. Patent and Trademark Office and in other countries. Marca Registrada. Bantam Books, 666 Fifth Avenue, New York, New York 10103.

PRINTED IN THE UNITED STATES OF AMERICA

O   0 9 8 7 6 5

CAMP
GIRL-MEETS-BOY

1

The day was bright and beautiful. Camp Menunkechogue looked like a picture postcard of rolling hills, clear lakefront, and happy campers. Between the long thin dock and the square yellow float fifty yards out, Marissa's Dolphins swam gracefully. The little girls kept stroking as Marissa shouted words of encouragement and praise. On shore it was a totally different story.

"Today," Violet said to her Cribbies, "we are supposed to learn to put our faces in the water."

Six Cribbies moaned and clutched each other. "I would rather eat last week's scrambled eggs," said one twelve-year-old firmly. The Cribbies, non-swimmers who were confined to a shallow area blocked off by red bobbers, shared the opinion that it was not shallow enough.

"And I agree," said Vi, "which is why I have located this hammock. The point of today's exercise will be that a girl can have great pleasure in the water simply by watching it. It is not necessary actually to touch water to enjoy it."

"Hurray!" shouted the Cribbies, and they hurled themselves into the wide rope hammock and swung happily, thus arousing considerable envy among the Dolphins, who noticed what was happening and asked their counselor why they couldn't have a hammock during swimming, too.

Vi stood on the sand in front of the hammock. From a distance (a great distance), it might have looked as if she were demonstrating swim strokes. She wasn't. She was dancing. Vi had the night off, and since there was a boys' camp on the far side of the lake, she was rehearsing. Unfortunately there had been no invitation from the boy counselors. Vi lacked the nerve just to paddle over all by herself. The only other counselor she knew well was Marissa, who hardly seemed a likely prospect to visit the other side of the lake for a strictly social purpose. Marissa probably spent her evenings off identifying leaves, or memorizing bear tracks.

Marissa was the one who brought a compass and canteen. Vi was the one whose eye shadow weighed so much the boys had to help her haul it up the cliff.

Marissa was the kind of counselor who thought that anything that happened at Camp Menunkechogue was good, and anyone who went there was good, and even any food they served there was good. Vi was the kind of counselor who brought —and hid—enough cheese Doodles to bribe her campers into rest-hour silence.

Marissa loved to sing the camp song, and all songs related to camp, and all songs with fifteen verses. Vi always wanted to know what kind of a name was Camp Menunkechogue, anyway. "Nothing rhymes with Menunkechogue," Violet complained when Marissa led singing. "Except maybe, *Go catch a hog.* Or, *How thick the smog.*"

Marissa loved how they were nestled in the woods at the top of the cliff. "Romantic cabins in the primeval forest," Marissa would breathe. Whereas Violet was opposed to trees. Especially trees all close together, their greenery joined at the top like a lid keeping in prisoners. Vi felt that Big Foot was just a step away.

That Marissa and Violet should be sharing responsibility for the twelve-year-old girls seemed to Vi one of those cruelties of fate that could not be justified. No matter how Vi tried, she could not make friends with Marissa, who practically wore a Superman cape instead of a beach towel. This summer Vi had more girlfriends than ever in her life—but they were all in elementary school.

A night off, thought Vi. It'll be like a precious gem I have to throw away because I don't know what to do with it.

A shadow crossed the sand, and the Cribbies shrank into their hammock. Vi looked up.

It was Charles, the owner of Camp Menunkechogue. Vi had not managed to make friends with Charles, either. He'd hired her, but somewhere along the way the lines of communication were cut.

On the very first day, Vi and Marissa had stood at the bottom of the cliff, each standing by her luggage. That was how Charles judged Vi and wondered if he'd made a mistake. Vi was actually surrounded by her luggage: she had several suitcases,

3

a trunk, two cases of makeup, and a carry-on bag full of paperbacks. Marissa had an olive green backpack—the real kind, not a book bag—and she was wearing it, and through the material, you could actually see the outline of hiking boots—the real kind, as if she actually intended to wear those thirty-pound shoes that gave you more blisters than cute little pink sneakers, anyway. Marissa also had a duffel bag that not only wasn't full, it wasn't even half full. The first thing Violet said to Marissa was, "How long are you planning to stay? Half an hour?"

Charles saw Vi's matching pastel blue luggage (in molded plastic, so nothing would crush) and asked, "Where are you planning to go on your evening off, Violet? France?"

That started the hostilities.

Real campers versus Violet. Charles, Marissa, and their camp-loving kind versus all the little girls who loved to try on Vi's eye shadow, or borrow her trays of nail polish, or practice setting their hair, or try on some of her vast wardrobe.

The second confrontation was over clothing. Camp Menunkechogue, better known as Camp Men, had regulations: solid shorts, Camp Men T-shirts, and for swimming, navy blue polyester tank suits. Violet could not bring herself to wear any of that. Charles yelled at her, "Didn't you read the list of clothing rules for counselors?"

Vi said, "Well, of course I read it. I didn't think you were serious, though."

There were several things at stake when Charles appeared on the sand. First, and most importantly, was that he would want the Cribbies in the water, and Vi had promised them a water-free lesson. She

4

didn't want to back down. Charles was winning every round, and she was sick of it. Second, Charles was threatening to take away her night off if she didn't "shape up." And third, and most important in view of summer fashion, Vi hated to get her dumb bathing suit wet. Nobody looked good in the tank suits. If you were big-busted, you fell out, and if you were flat-chested, the suit sagged in a poly-ester puddle. Although there was not a boy in sight, and the girls looked identical in the dreadful suits, Vi liked to look her best at all times and in all places. So she said, "Hi, there, Charles, Come join us."

Charles looked wary.

"We're building self-esteem," said Vi, figuring no camp owner could argue with self-esteem.

Charles snorted. "You just don't want to get your mascara wet, Violet."

"My mascara is waterproof, of course," snapped Vi.

One of Vi's campers, Claudia, had left the hammock to stand beside Vi. She began patting Vi gently. Claudia was twelve and therefore more mature and relaxed than Vi, and often helped Vi keep her perspective on things.

"I'm glad," said Charles. "At least your mascara won't come off with all the rest of your makeup and mousse and perfume and polish, and pollute my lake."

Vi was furious. She used only the highest grades of everything. In fact, this was proving to be a very expensive summer, what with sharing with all the little girls. She occasionally thought Marissa, who shared only knowledge and enthusiasm, had the better idea. She said to Charles, "Your lake is already so polluted no sensible girl would put her face in it anyway."

Charles began yelling, "My lake? Polluted? This is northern Maine! I'll have you know lakes are not polluted here!"

Claudia murmured, "Vi, Vi, remember we still have cabin inspection to go. If we don't pass, you won't get your night off."

"This," shouted Charles, "is a sparkling fresh diamond in an emerald green wilderness."

Vi twisted curls around her finger while she considered her next move. Swim period was half gone. A long time left to continue hostilities with Charles. Vi was not basically a hostile person. She much preferred friendly banter, or flirting, although Charles was a hundred and not worthy of her time. Vi looked longingly across the lake where the boys' camp was. *They* were worth her time!

Charles transferred his attention to her hair. "Have you been using those appliances again?"

He made it sound as if she had brought a pasta maker and a blender. Vi had brought only the absolute essentials: her hot rollers, curling iron, blow dryer, lighted makeup mirror, contact-lens heater, and so forth.

"If you leave any of those plugged in, Vi," said Charles, his eyebrows gripping each other like fierce little fighters, "and your cabin catches fire, and my campers and all the animals of the forest have to flee, and—"

"I am not going to murder anybody, Charles!" yelled Violet. "I am just going to have curly hair, all right?"

6

With New England speed, the weather changed. Thunderclouds boiled up and whipped past Lost Loon Mountain and sped over Charles's lake. Out in the water, Marissa blew a sharp warning on her whistle, and the Dolphins swam powerfully to shore. Violet held out her hand and caught the first drop. "Hmph!" she said to Charles with a pixie smile. "Acid rain. Come on, girls, let's run."

Marissa loved rainy days.

Nobody could entertain little girls indoors better than Marissa.

The last time it rained, she had told a terrific lost-in-the-forest story, where every girl was assigned a specific noise: Claudia did the scream, Laury did the burp, Janey did the waterfall. Everybody was jealous of Laury.

The time before, Marissa had organized an early Halloween and gave green pumpkins to the winners of the costume categories. (It was not easy to make fascinating costumes out of Camp Men T-shirts and regulation tank suits, so Vi's cabin had had an unfair advantage: trunks of designer clothing and unlimited makeup.) The green pumpkins were actually watermelons. After the costume parade, they had had a dinosaur-egg hunt in the rain. The dinosaur eggs were the same watermelons, and after the hunt, of course, they had had a seed-spitting contest.

Today Marissa had the girls clear all the tables in the dining hall to one side and stack the chairs on top. Chilly wind blew in the huge screened windows that wrapped the hall, but the wide porches

7

protected them from rain. Outside the sky was black, the waves steel gray, the trees dark silhouettes, and the long thin deck a fragile stick beneath the storm.

Inside, Marissa lined up the girls in long rows, each row six feet apart. Then she unrolled a vast length of wide brown paper, gave everybody colored chalk and crayons, and every other girl lay down to have her outline traced by the girl behind her. Then they traded places and in a few minutes, every girl was drawn on the paper. They wrote their names beneath their outlines, and Marissa got out her stopwatch. "Okay, everybody," she yelled. "Move on three silhouettes! Stop! Now you have thirty seconds in which to add hair to the drawing in front of you."

Little girls dropped to their knees, screaming, "But I only have navy blue crayon!" "But I don't know what Celia's hair looks like!" "But I wanted to do my own hair!"

"Time's up!" shrieked Marissa. "Move on!"

By the time the portraits were done, and the brown paper taped on the walls, the storm had ended. The girls put out the tables again, and stood on them, and the tallest girls were able to tape the rest of the silhouettes to the ceiling. Autographs, questionable poems, pointed reminders to bunkmates, and caricatures of Charles had already been added in the spaces, but there was room for lots more.

Charles held Violet's cabin responsible for the more vulgar remarks penned on the mural. "Just because I have unnaturally curly hair," shrieked Violet, "does not mean I would write *that* on the wall!"

Marissa stared at Vi.

How was she supposed to be friends with this irresponsible fluffball? This creature who had brought enough clothes to travel first class on the *QE2*?

Camp. O Camp.

For Marissa, it was a heartsong.

School, crummy old school, was nothing but a void between summers. But *camp!*

Sunshine on the beloved lake. The intoxicating scent of fir trees around the cabin. The laughter of friends, a forehead whacked on the bunk above. Campfire in the dark, girls swaying as they sang. Marshmallows getting soft on their twigs in the flame, waiting for the luscious moment when you squished them between two graham crackers and two pieces of Hershey's chocolate, and sank your teeth into the season's first S'more.

Buddies at swimming . . . buddies on hikes . . . buddies for crafts . . . all these buddies who never, never, never wrote over the winter. Funny how you used the word *buddy* only at camp. You couldn't do anything without your buddy. Buddies might be assigned or chosen, but everything was a three-legged race. Camp assumption was that nothing could go wrong, no safety rules be broken, as long as you had a buddy.

Every summer, Marissa looked forward to the new buddies and the old. Girls who shared years of memories, and girls who shared none. Girls who knew every verse of every camp song, and girls who didn't.

Buddies? With Violet?

Violet didn't even have a real name, or real shoes, let alone a real personality.

9

Charles was lecturing the campers. He had an unfortunate tendency to run on. Other summers, Marissa had found it rather endearing. Now she just got itchy.

"Wonderful job," said Charles. "I know we're going to enjoy this beautiful mural all summer. Thank you, Marissa. Wonderful job, as always, Marissa."

He pointed to her, as if nobody had met her before, and the girls clapped. Marissa could not help looking to see if Vi was clapping. Marissa was trying to set an example of good camp-counselor behavior for Vi. She thought it was just as well that Vi kept her Cribbies on the sand. Otherwise they might drown around her ankles, because Vi would be too busy scanning the horizon for cute boys to notice them.

Boys, thought Marissa.

There was only one boy in her dreams.

She was horrified to find tears rising, and had to tilt her head up to keep them from overflowing. She pretended to be admiring the drawing right above her.

"Now we'll have lunch, girls," said Charles. "And during rest hour today I know you'll be writing your letters home, and I will see you again to-morrow."

The girls chorused, "Oh, no!"

Charles thought they were sorry he was going. He gave them a lengthy explanation about how he had two camps to run: their brother camp, Camp Menunkechogue for Boys, needed him, too.

Of course they were just telling him they had no

intention of wasting a perfectly good rest hour by writing home.

Marissa swallowed hard.

Camp, lovely camp, was no more than an unrequited crush on a boy across the lake, and jealousy over a counselor who broke all the rules.

Her first night off. And what was she supposed to do with it? Write home? What was she supposed to say?

I wish I hadn't come.

2

---

*T*here were times when Alicia, the camp nurse, loved her job, and times when it was the most boring task on earth. Campers and counselors were notoriously healthy. So far today she had agreed that sunburns did hurt, that it was better not to pick poison ivy for the camp table bouquet, and that when dared to pick up a can lid with one's tongue, perhaps one should say no.

Alicia wanted more out of camp life than that. She looked up the camp schedule to see whose night off it was. Marissa and Vi. Poor Charles was having trouble with Vi. Alicia could whip Vi into shape, so this was good: she would have a night off and deal with a difficult counselor. Alicia liked the efficient sound of this.

When the lunch bell rang, she went cheerfully for her macaroni and cheese. The campers were so exhausted they could barely hoist their forks. Vi's table wanted to know if they could omit forks entirely and just put their faces down in the plates and lap up lunch. Vi thought this was an interesting idea.

Alicia, as the adult present, said it was interesting, but it was also not allowed. "At camp," she said firmly, "we maintain our standards."

"We have standards," said Claudia, speaking for Vi's group. "It's just that they're very low."

The girls giggled uncontrollably. Vi said they were going to ruin her reputation. The girls said what reputation?

Alicia patrolled Vi's table to keep faces out of food.

After rest hour, Marissa would split the Minnows into two groups, and they would have Ping-Pong relays: blowing the Ping-Pong ball between two buoys and swimming after it for eight exchanges. The future teams were screaming at each other, "We're going to cream you!" "We'll slaughter you!"

And the horseback-riding class, which was going on a trail ride this afternoon, was begging to be allowed just to ride, and not have to notice anything. "I hate noticing things," moaned Claudia. "Do we really have to look at the woods? Can't we just ride around?"

Alicia apparently felt that with all this going on, she could speak privately to two counselors. "Marissa?" said Alicia sweetly. "Vi?"

If their counselors were going to get yelled at, the campers wanted to listen.

"Would you like to go with me in the Jeep over to the boys' side of the lake after supper?" asked Alicia. "You both have the night off."

If Alicia had hoped this remark would be covered by the sound of macaroni and cheese going down a hundred and fifty throats, she was mistaken. Campers loved gossip much more than nature, and it was about time that Marissa and Violet actually did something.

"Yes!" shrieked Vi's cabin. "They would! There are boys over there. Vi has a crush on Dark! Who do you have a crush on, Marissa? They want to go kissing, Alicia. Tell us what happens, Alicia!"

Alicia was tiny and doll-like, but not cuddly: she was more a china doll than a rag doll. She lacked Marissa's excitement and Vi's craziness. Marissa dressed like a camp counselor and Vi like a model, but Alicia resembled Mary Poppins: slick black hair, rosy red cheeks, firm movements, and a wrist she flicked like an umbrella.

Vi's cabin began cheering, and there was much ringing of metal spoons against half-empty glasses.

She had to say it at lunch, thought Marissa, with my whole cabin here. And when I get in tonight at midnight, they'll all be awake and giggling and they'll want details.

Which would be fine as long as there *were* details.

If Marissa could say—"None of your business; go back to sleep!"—all the while hugging the romantic truth to herself—well, then, it was okay. But what if nothing happened? What if they drove over there and none of the boys had time off? Or they had a night off but didn't want to spend it with Marissa? Or the great boys like Sin and Dark weren't free, but the creepy ones like fat old Rick or weedy old Scotty were?

"We'll pick out what you wear, Marissa," said

14

her cabin firmly. They had their image to worry about and they didn't want Marissa going off in a Camp Men T-shirt.

"And we'll put on your makeup for you," said Vi's cabin.

Alicia said the campers would stick with the normal camp schedule rather than attending Marissa and Violet in their dressing rooms.

"Dressing room," said Claudia happily. "That's what we'll call our cabin now, Vi. The Dressing Room."

Marissa wondered uneasily just what would happen once she and Vi and Alicia had acquired a Jeep and a night off. The village was six miles away. Of course there wasn't much there, just a gas station, two inns, a hunting/fishing supply store, a church, another church now being used as a pottery, and three antique shops. It was not easy to find non-camp entertainment in northern Maine. What if when they finally arrived at the boys' camp the boys all flirt with Vi? thought Marissa. And they never even notice me?

Rest hour.

Vi looked forward to rest hour the way she used to look forward to Christmas.

She had three requests of Santa Claus: first, that her cabin (which never rested; it was a miracle to Vi her campers weren't all in comas from all their activity) would rest today. She needed her beauty sleep. Vi had all the girls with insomnia. Girls who thought nothing of imitating rats at two in the morning. Girls who had M & M's fights at three in

15

the morning. Girls who wanted to find out who could eat the most shoelaces at four in the morning. With nights like that, you needed naps by day.

Her second request was that at least one boy at Camp Men would fall in love with her.

And her third was that Laury would not wet the bed today when she fell asleep.

This had not been part of Vi's bargain in camp counseling. She had been prepared for all the rest when Charles gave the counselors the opening night lecture. She nodded proudly along with every teenager there: yes, yes, no problem. I can be teacher, coach, psychologist, sports authority, swimming instructor, storyteller, folksinger, forest ranger, and crafts specialist.

Piece of cake.

But Charles neglected to mention that she might have to change sheets, air a mattress, drink in the smell of urine, protect Laury from the laughter of the other girls, and pretend it was all perfectly routine. Vi did not think it was routine at all. Vi thought it was ghastly.

"All right, you guys!" yelled Vi. "Write your letters!" She knew perfectly well nobody was going to write a letter home.

Claudia's father was divorcing Claudia's mother to marry Heather Anne, and Claudia's mother, for revenge, was going to marry Claudia's father's partner Jonathan, and Claudia was going to have to be the bridesmaid at two weddings in September. Claudia had nothing to say to either parent, and if she mailed them anything it would be a hand grenade.

Janey, as far as Vi could tell, had not yet conquered the alphabet, which made letter writing quite a task. Janey usually paid Claudia to write her postcards instead.

As for Laury, she routinely wrote to her hamster. "My parents are too busy," she said, "my brother stinks, and the dog is always off chasing cats. So there's only the hamster to write to, anyway."

The cabin did not quiet down.

Vi tucked herself into a ball on her bed, shoving armloads of clutter to the floor. The cabin was rather full. On the few shelves were baseball mitts, tissue boxes, comic books, unused writing paper, dried-up pens, cameras, and sunglasses. Hanging from nails were sneakers tied by the laces and teddy bears strangling on neck ribbons. Tacked on walls were rock-star posters, and gathered in teetering stacks were cassettes. The pride of the cabin was a stolen train sign which read Do Not Flush at Station. ("And did you?" everybody always excitedly asked.)

"Sssssshhh!" hissed Vi. "Do you want Marissa down here yelling at us again?"

Nobody wanted Marissa down there yelling at them again. Their cabin was a special territory, like nothing the campers had ever shared before, and Vi was their special crazy property. They whispered, "Tell us another story about the Green-Eyed Maniac, Vi. Please? Pretty please? Please with a cherry and whipped cream on top?"

"No. You'll scream."

They promised her not to scream.

Vi lay on her back and stared at the ceiling. Her girls had taken the little cereal boxes from breakfast and fastened them to the ceiling with double-side tape. At first they placed them in rows (Sugar Smacks, then Froot Loops, then Cheerios), but they got bored and just stuck them up any old which way. Luckily, during inspection, Charles never glanced up.

Vi was partial to horror stories in which the Green-Eyed Maniac captured little girls and suffocated them between bunk-bed mattresses which automatically lowered during the night.

". . . but when she peered between the dusty slats of the venetian blinds out into the misty ghost-ridden night," whispered Vi, "the poor little camper looked straight into the twisted face and hypnotic eyes of the Green-Eyed Maniac!"

Janey screamed. Claudia threw a pillow at her. And Laury wet the bed.

Another typical rest hour.

Marissa wondered if Violet was worried, too, or if all Vi's experiences with boys had been happy and worry-free. Marissa still got panic-stricken over the mere thought of dating. Give her a mountain hike any day.

By supper Marissa was a wreck. It offended her. This was camp. If there was any place on earth where you should be exempt from scary social situations, it was surely a wilderness camp in Maine. It did not help that she was going out with a girl who practically took eye-shadow baths.

They left the Dressing Room together and slid on down toward the road. The lake glittered like black diamonds in the night, and the lights from the boys' side twinkled distantly. "You know what I'm wondering?" said Vi. "What boy over there is Alicia interested in?"

"Alicia?" gasped Marissa. "She's a hundred! She can't be interested in any of those boys."

"She's probably not even thirty. And some of the counselors are in their twenties."

Marissa was aghast at the thought. Alicia seemed incredibly old to her, and very nursey. Vi looked darling in pink-and-yellow-splashed cotton, with the perfect accessories and lipstick. Marissa felt stodgy and dull. The jeep pulled up and Marissa climbed into the front seat. Alicia was wearing a dress of white cotton, looking extra doll-like: flirty and summery. She did not look like an old nurse at all; she looked like a young bridesmaid.

Marissa would have climbed right out of the Jeep, except that Claudia was racing by and stopped to wish them all good luck.

"Good luck at what?" said Alicia, puzzled.

"Getting boys," said Marissa glumly.

Alicia smiled to herself, and no longer looked puzzled.

3

Alicia drove very slowly.

Marissa adored driving and worshipped speed. She loved anything with a noisy motor: speedboats, motorcycles, souped-up cars. She even once took domestic science in high school and sat racing the sewing machine engine instead of hemming her apron project. She could hardly even sit in the Jeep while Alicia puddled along. She locked her fingers together so she wouldn't rip the wheel out of Alicia's dainty hands.

Vi, who disliked the forest at night, also wanted to go faster. Because at this speed, almost anything might climb into the open Jeep with them. Lions and tigers and bears, she thought. Green-eyed maniacs. Bats and wolverines and rapists. She sat alone in back and stared at Alicia's and Marissa's hair.

Marissa's was fastened in a long, narrow double comb and lay like a wild horse's mane against her neck. From the front she looked businesslike: hair out of the way like a good swim instructor. But from the side, oh, she looked incredibly romantic: tumbling thick dark curls. Both her own cabin, Sunset, and the Dressing Room had passed approval on her hair.

Vi was filled with nagging doubts and envy that she was ashamed of. Marissa was so calm, so good at everything. But Vi had always felt more feminine. Now she could see this was ridiculous. Marissa had just been dressing sturdily for sturdy occasions. Tonight, in a simple blue-black shirt, and stone-washed jeans with a row of narrow tucks, and that wonderful dark hair cascading down her back, she was stunning.

Vi felt like the classic dumb blond.

Alicia's hair was pulled tightly back into the neatest twist in America. Her lipstick was very red, her earrings were white jet bangles, and she had a prim bridal-shower prettiness that, just because it was so out of place, was fascinating.

Vi would have preferred to sit there worrying about monsters (including the monster of jealousy rising up inside), but Alicia said in a warm kind voice, "Are you enjoying camp, dear?"

"Yes."

"And do you enjoy your little campers, dear?"

"Yes."

Alicia stopped as if there were an octagonal red stop sign in the middle of the forest. Vi's pulse doubled as she waited for grizzly bears and escaped murderers to crawl out of the dark. Alicia turned in the front seat to look Vi full in the face. "I've

21

been wondering lately, Vi. Why on earth did you become a counselor, anyway?"

Of course, some people probably went to camp in order to get fresh air, or mosquito bites, or swim in a lake, but she, Violet, she personally, planned to go in order to meet boys.

When Violet was twelve, and all the boys she knew were ghastly, her cousin Gretchen was a counselor at Camp Menunkechogue. Gretchen had met Michael there, and last year Violet got to be a bridesmaid at their wedding and carry lilies of the valley and white roses. Gretchen (who never learned to pronounce the name of her own camp) had always referred to the place as Camp Girl-Meets-Boy.

It became Violet's ambition to spend a summer at Camp Girl-Meets-Boy and to meet a boy of her own.

She had to remember to call it Camp Menunkechogue in public, because people (especially boys) were surprised to find that Camp Girl-Meets-Boy was an actual place, and they always wanted to know exactly what it was that the counselors supervised at such a camp.

Gretchen would explain that, due to pronunciation problems with the Indian syllables, everybody there just called it Camp Men. And that suited Violet fine: Camp Men.

How clearly she imagined all those men, astride their tall chestnut horses, flinging dark hair out of their eyes, off to rappel down cliffs and white-water canoe a few rapids, perhaps start a campfire with flint, and very likely finish the day with a square dance, featuring her—Violet—as the most popular girl at camp.

In her daydreams, Violet hardly ever thought of the campers themselves. She herself had gone to day camp for three summers and then last year had been shipped off for two weeks to Camp Ragged Rock, where she rode horses or played computer games. Vi could not recall any counselors, but there must have been some, as it was surely illegal to run a camp without them.

At any rate, on the seventeenth day of June, Violet had her suitcases ready, her hair curled, and her heart waiting.

The boys definitely came up to all her expectations.

There was Sin, who was tan and golden and suave and sophisticated. She adored Sin right away. He was such a city kid, and yet somehow he fit right into camp as if he belonged. Sin was the kind of person who could be country ten weeks and no more; by then he needed to put on a suit, go to the theater, and drive a Jaguar. Violet was definitely willing to have Sin.

There was Jamie, who did mowing and maintenance. Jamie wore, exclusively, cutoff jeans. Never a shirt. Violet watched Jamie ride the huge mower every time the grass got high. (That was the one good thing about all this rain that kept them in the common room and Marissa racking her brain for entertainment: the grass grew a lot.) Jamie's crewcut hair was so short he just bristled. Normally Vi disapproved of crewcuts, but Jamie was adorable, like a great big teddy bear, and Vi longed to ride the mower with him. Jamie liked to tell people he was a native Maine boy, just a townie, a born woodsman, but in fact he was from Queens, in New York, and had learned all he knew about the great outdoors and lawnmower repair right here at Camp Men.

It was Dark, however, on whom Vi had set her sights.

She had gotten the phrase *set your sights* from Claudia, her camper, who was taking riflery. Claudia, whose family was busy divorcing and remarrying, said she felt better shooting rifles than lying around getting tan, which Violet thought was a little spooky, but anyway, Vi had set her sights for Dark.

Dark had not responded as yet, but Vi would have been a little disappointed if he had. Dark was mysterious and difficult. If he had a real name he wasn't telling. Handsome and silent, black-eyed and brown-haired—if there was ever a boy who belonged in a wilderness camp, it was this one. Violet loved that in a guy: where they were full of mysteries and secrets. She could see Dark climbing cliffs or skydiving or riding horseback to the rescue.

Dark, however, was the computer expert. There was no romance in computers. Vi had been forced to take keyboarding at high school. She did not have a flair for it. Many a class period, she had dreamed of lifting her keyboard high in the air and smashing it against a convenient skull. "You're too tan to be an indoor sportsman," she told Dark, but he just smiled.

He had a mysterious smile: one that she had

24

stood in front of a mirror and tried to imitate, but couldn't. The right half of his mouth smiled beautifully and the left half did nothing. Vi's campers said he looked as if he'd had a stroke. But Vi thought the twisted smile was the sexiest she'd ever seen.

There was only one problem with all these fine young men. They stayed on the other side of the lake, counseling little boys, while she was stuck on this side, changing Laury's sheets and taping cereal boxes to the ceiling.

And she was always getting in trouble, when what she wanted to do was get in a car with Jamie, or Dark, or Sin.

She could get into trouble over anything.

The other day Marissa had a sweet little activity: everybody had to make up a new camp song for future camp generations to sing in remembrance of this special summer.

Marissa's group composed:

> *Some people like computer printouts*
> *Some people like bugs*
> *Some people like hotdogs with*
>   *mustard*
> *Some people like hugs*
> *But I love Camp Men!*
> *I'll come again and again!*

Violet's girls wrote:

> *Summer brings joy to every heart*
> *Nobody gets to stay apart*

Especially if they wet the bed
Or have lice on their head.

Alicia freaked out when Laury, Janey, Claudia, and the others bellowed those lyrics. "Nobody has lice!" she screamed, but just to be sure, she made them have a head check that very night, and of course everybody held Violet entirely responsible.

But the surprise—the emotion that startled so she sometimes stayed awake even during rest hour—was that Violet loved camp.

Not the counselors, not the boys, not the campers, not the food—but camp itself.

She yearned for campfire just like Marissa. She loved dusk, when the stars glittered above the lake, and the lake surface turned soft and velvety, and the embers died down, voices dwindled, and life was good.

She loved watching Marissa. Marissa flung herself into activities like a teenage boy into his first car. Marissa loved everything: bird songs and marsh grass, cloud formations and flag raising, volleyball tournaments and parents' day.

Violet had never been around anybody so enthusiastic, and in fact, Vi had trained her cabin to laugh at Marissa. But now she was ashamed. She caught herself imitating Marissa instead of ogling boys; she found herself wondering not what Jamie or Sin or Dark would think . . . but what Marissa would think.

Violet stared out of the Jeep into the dark woods. It occurred to her that she would not be nervous

if Marissa had been driving, because lions and tigers and bears would never bother Marissa. Violet
said to Alicia, "Oh, you know. I thought I'd make
friends. Learn to take responsibility. See Maine.
Stuff like that."

4

Alicia started the Jeep up again. The road was very rutted. They bounced painfully. "Marissa, you were a camper for six years yourself, weren't you?"

"Yes," said Marissa. She knew Vi had chosen not to tell Alicia anything. But then, Vi hadn't told Marissa anything, either. She doesn't trust us, thought Marissa. I haven't been very nice. I've judged her on everything: her makeup, mostly. And what did she do with that makeup? The very first day, when Claudia was trying to run after her father and make him not marry Heather Anne after all, Vi got Claudia to stay by coaxing her to try on purple eye shadow and matching nail polish.

A better offer than mine would have been. I was going to take Claudia on a walk in the pines and talk about families.

Let's be real here. Anybody would rather have shiny purple nails than talk about truth.

Alicia said, "And why did you become a counselor, Marissa?"

Camp. O Camp!
This was the year, long awaited, that Marissa turned sixteen and could be a counselor instead of a camper. Far more exciting than getting her driver's license or her own checking account.

On the first day, Vi had accused Marissa of carrying nothing. The real burden Marissa shouldered was her very first crush.

A first crush is extra precious because of what comes before it: the worry that you might never have one, that there is something wrong with you, that your town does not feature a single boy worthy of a crush, and that you are doomed.

Marissa had been interested in boys only because her girlfriends were. The boys she knew were duds and not half the company her girlfriends were. But nobody else felt like that, and Marissa wanted to be in step, so she claimed to love boys, too. But she was lying. And it upset her. And she looked forward to Camp Men as the one place, contrary to the nickname, where there were no men to worry about.

Camp Menunkechogue required her to be interviewed. Charles could not fit Marissa into his schedule, so she was to be interviewed by Sinclair ("Call me Sin") Franklin. Sin was two years older than Marissa and, like her, had been a camper at Camp Men. Sin of course had gone to the boys' camp across the lake, but the two camps shared some activities, horseback riding being the one both Marissa and Sin took. Horses tended to be a girls' kind of activity, and girls who adored horses usually despised boys. Marissa was no exception and had for years regarded Sin as an interloper spoiling everything.

This year, actually, Charles had added another coed activity to the camp agenda—computers. It disgusted Marissa. What decent American parents would send their kid to the Maine woods in order to sit indoors typing at a computer terminal? She pictured a weedy, wasted computer hack, his glasses on sideways and his complexion popping like breakfast cereal. Furthermore, the computers were housed in the common room, the only building with a reliable roof. Marissa regarded this as a trespass: the common room was for butterfly collections, stunts in the evening, and sing-alongs. Not for hardware, software, and boys.

But who showed up to teach computers? A dark, handsome, intense athlete about whom nobody would talk. Charles wouldn't talk about him, Sin wouldn't talk about him, and the first evening of orientation when Violet interrogated him he backed into the shadows, so Vi had begun giggling. "I am truly in the dark about you," she had said. And after that they called him Dark, and Dark introduced himself that way even to the parents.

Marissa tried to flirt with Dark, but either she did not know how or he was not interested. Marissa did not know which would be a worse reason.

At any rate, old Sin had interviewed Marissa. Marissa was amazed to find that she and Sin lived only eleven miles apart. Like so many camps, Menunkechogue drew its campers from a particular geographical area; in this case, New York City and Westchester County, New York. But when you were in northern Maine, wrapped in the vast wilderness of pine trees and silver brooks, you never thought you might have a second neighborhood in common.

Marissa had dressed up for the interview because her mother made her. "It isn't camp yet," said her mother, "and you do possess a skirt, Marissa. Now try to look like a human being for the interview." Her mother was tired of blue jeans, which her daughter wore three hundred sixty-four days of the year, the exception being the day of the music concert when she had worn a band uniform (scarlet, with gold epaulets). Her mother had taken a hundred photographs that day, since it was Marissa's first presentable moment in all of high school.

So Marissa had worn a pink blouse, and matching long skirt made of very thin sweatshirt material: clingy, and yet lots of fabric that swayed like a light wind whenever she moved. The white belt emphasized how slender she was.

Sin had said, "You know, Mariss, I don't think I ever saw you in a skirt before. You look excellent. Funny how people are strictly camp in memory, isn't it? I see you exclusively in the Camp Men T-shirt with the sun rising over your—uh—" Sin stumbled and blushed. The T-shirt was designed so that the golden sun logo lay right on the chest: flat on the boys, rising on the older girls. "Anyway," said Sin, turning around quickly and heading for the safety of his living room—and Cokes— "you look great."

She immediately had a crush on Sin so bad she

31

thought she might attack him. It came from no-
where, so fierce she had to hang on to the pillow
in the easy chair. By the end of the evening she
was holding the pillow in her lap, hugging and
caressing it.

In spite of the fact that it was early spring and
very chilly out, Sin had been wearing his navy
shorts and Camp Men T-Shirt. He had exceedingly
wide shoulders, wide enough so that his extra-
large shirt fit him only in the shoulders and from
there hung like a tent to his thighs. In summer,
he would be darkly tanned, nose slathered with
zinc, eyes hidden by wraparound sunglasses. She
suddenly remembered Sin had thick blond hair
on his chest, like white sea foam against a golden
wave.

"You'll be teaching the advanced swimmers, of
course," said Sin. All she could think of was that
Sin brought the boys over by boat, the ones taking
horseback riding or computer. I'll see Sin every
day, she had thought.

With loathing she remembered that nasty tank
suit. Why, oh why couldn't she wear her bikini?
Marissa was clumsy on land, but beautiful in water.
She loved to dive in, swim underwater a long way,
surface with a shake of her head, and see everybody else holding their breath, impressed.

Perhaps Charles would allow an exception to the
tank suit rule.

Marissa laughed at herself. Charles would never
allow an exception. Part of what camp *was* was no
exceptions. Campers were all alike: in T-shirts, activities, bedtimes, and food. It was one of the ways

in which camp was so much more wonderful than school. You could excel—say, placing Dolphin in swimming rather than Minnow—but you could not differ. There was a sense of community, of intimacy, at camp that you never felt at school, where people went a hundred different ways.

Sin had asked Marissa the questions required by the form that Charles had given him, "Do you like outdoors activities?" said Sin sternly.

They had both giggled. Only Marissa would interrupt the rhythm of canoeing to announce what kind of insects were hovering by the marsh grass.

"You are going to be such an asset to the Camp," Sin had said, smiling. "Charles told me you'll have Sunset Cabin, and a counselor named Violet will have Sunrise, and you'll be the one in charge."

Her first summer as a full-fledged counselor, and she had all the twelve-year-old girls. To think that Charles had such faith in her! "Oh, Sin," she had said joyously. Marissa was so sick of being a teenager. Having to take instructions, always saying *Yes, Mummy, Yes, Teacher*. Enough! She wanted to be an adult.

Sunset Cabin was her favorite: on the edge of a hill so high that parents gulped and warned their daughters not to fall off. The sun drenched the cabin by day, and in the evening the forest, which crept right up to the rocky precipice and whose branches rasped against the cabin walls at night, cast long lacy shadows over the little wooden porch. Raccoons came out at night and wandered around. Marissa had had a counselor once who told the girls the noise was made by a bear. Everybody had screamed in happy fear. Marissa thought that maybe she too would say it was bears.

You needed a bear or two to make it really Maine.

My cabin! thought Marissa. *Cabins*, actually, since I'll be in charge of Sunrise, too.

When the interview was over, Sin and Marissa had walked awkwardly to the door. Sin had looked at the hall wallpaper—shiny black and silver pentagons—and then at the hall floor—glossy black and white marble tiles. It was a very citified room: a decorator's achievement. Nothing could have been more of a contrast to Camp Menunkechogue.

" 'Bye, Sin," Marissa had said. She yearned to touch him but didn't dare extend even a hand. She wanted him to ask her out, or ask her to stay, or offer her another Coke: anything to make the moment last. She had even thought of leaving her purse behind so she would have to come back for it.

She had studied his eyes, because come summer they would stay behind the sunglasses he favored. She had studied how his extra-large shirt hung and imagined the muscles beneath it and then quickly studied the black-and-white tiles before he could read her mind.

And Sin had hugged her good-bye.

It was a quick hug: a hug of friendship and an-ticipation about the summer, but Marissa hadn't wanted to move even her elbows after that, trying to save the feel of Sin's arms wrapping her.

"See you in June," he had said.

Marissa spent the last six weeks of school hoping

the phone would ring: that Sin would ask her to his prom, or to the movies, or even to help out at his school's carwash, but of course he didn't.

Marissa dreamed of the first day of camp: the day before the campers arrived—the day when all the boys' counselors and all the girls' counselors met for planning sessions, for ordering supplies, for agreeing on play scripts and the lake-use schedule and who would chaperone which hiking and canoeing trip.

The day before her father drove her to Westchester County Airport for her flight to Maine, Marissa had stood for hours in the bathroom, staring at her reflection. She had her own bathroom and dressing room. ("Much good it did us to build that for you," grumbled her mother) with pale pink tiles and cream-colored tub and lace-trimmed towels.

At camp they referred to the girls' lavatories as the Perch, because the toilets were on high wooden pedestals, as if they really *were* thrones. Hardly anybody's feet touched the ground when they went. The shower room was called the Rain Forest. One of the showers couldn't be turned off, and it kept hissing away all day. The Rain Forest was so damp you could hardly breathe in there for the moisture.

Marissa had looked forward to all the gossip you got at the Rain Forest or the Perch.

She had suddenly known that she wanted to *be* the gossip.

She wanted her twelve-year-olds to wonder about her and Sin the way once she had wondered about

35

her counselors. *Are they dating? Did he kiss her? What do you think they do on their nights off?*

Marissa stared at Alicia's lovely manicured hands. "Oh, you know," she said vaguely, "I like camp."

5

___

*T*hey arrived at the entrance to the boys' camp. Harsh winter storms had ripped down the matching entrance on the girls' side, but here a tall hewn-log portal straddled the rutted road, and twigs painted white formed the letters of Camp Menunkechogue. A brillantly white half moon lit a blue-gray sky. The boys had much more level ground than the girls, and their cabins were tucked into the woods in a large horseshoe around the open playing fields. Squarely in the center were their tennis courts. The high wire-enclosures glinted threateningly in the moonlight.

The lake lay like molten silver, and the tall pines on the opposite shore were eerily reflected in the water, tips, like fingers, trying to cross the lake and catch hold of the dock.

Canoes like giants' toe shoes were pulled up on the grass. White Clorox bottles on ropes that marked off the beginners' swimming area bobbed like ghost seals in the sea. Twisted evergreens fought among

37

wild rocks, and their silhouettes rose grotesquely black against the silver water.

Violet didn't see how anybody could go to the bathroom at night. How could you pass such horrifying shadows? Her own slippery path and the Perch seemed comforting and friendly in comparison.

Vi shivered. Maine nights were cold. Her pretty pink jacket was useless.

When she climbed out of the Jeep she could see the dock, stretching out into the reaching fingers reflected on the water. Where Violet had pictured couples in love dangling their toes in the water, kissing beneath the moon, a pile of life jackets glowed like radioactive oranges.

Violet turned. Both Marissa and Alicia were gone. And behind the Jeep was not a camp cabin, but a huge black Victorian house. A house of many rooms, sharp-edged and jutting, the rim of the forest exactly even with the railings of the porch. The trees swallowing the house, thick leaves reaching down for a last gulp.

White skirts flickered at the door. There was a muted slam. A loon out on the lake rasped its haunted desperate cry. Something flew in Violet's face and caught momentarily in her hair. She chewed back a scream and brushed wildly, and the bat flew on.

And a heavy, cold hand closed on Violet's neck.

Violet had always wondered if she would scream —or would she be paralyzed by fear—when her life was in danger? There was no longer any question. She would scream. Violet's scream ripped through the night like an air-raid siren before the bomb.

The door of the Victorian house was flung open. A screaming Marissa and a screaming Alicia raced toward Violet. Boys poured out of the dining hall, the cabins, and the showers.

"What's happening?"

"Who got hurt?"

"Is it a fire?"

As a hundred and fifty boys charged to the rescue, wonderful, handsome, mysterious Dark looked at Violet in horror. "Vi, I knocked a bat off your shoulder. I didn't dismember you and shove you up a chimney."

Dark in the dark. She should have known. Somebody turned on the floodlights used for night games. She would never need rouge again. Her cheeks were going to be permanently stained red.

"*Your* cheeks?" said Marissa afterward. "What about *my* cheeks? You think *I* wasn't a little embarrassed?"

"I was jumpy," said Vi. So much for her crush on Dark. If he ever saw Vi coming again, Dark would climb a tree and pretend to be a squirrel. "I didn't even find out Dark's name," she said mournfully.

"You don't deserve to know Dark's name!" hollered Marissa. In her whole life she would never forget standing there while a hundred and fifty boys and all their counselors laughed out loud at them. She could live through hurricanes, tornadoes, revolutions, and bears—but humiliation in front of boys—never. Little boys with freckles and braces laughed, older boys with pencil-thin legs

39

and scrawny chests laughed, adorable eight-year-olds and handsome eighteen-year-olds laughed.

Charles, who thought at the very least his beloved camp was burning down, was still shaking. Alicia was in her nurse mode, ready to give CPR. "I should have expected this from a girl with enough makeup to launch a Broadway show," said Charles. Eight-year-olds stomped their feet in disappointment. "There isn't even any blood," they complained. "With all that screaming, we figured there'd be lots of blood."

"Next time," promised Charles.

Great, thought Violet. If I ever scream again, Charles will kill me.

"Well, what do you expect?" said the eight-year-olds. "A girl," they added in disgust. "Girls are like that."

Marissa was practically puffing smoke. Oh, it made her so mad! Hundreds of calm, strong, intelligent girls, and the camp had to be represented by Violet, who was literally screaming about her own shadow. "Girls are *not* like that!" Marissa shouted.

"The evidence," said Dark, grinning, "is to the contrary." Dark began laughing. He had a great laugh. All her life Vi would regret losing Dark. You could definitely spend forever with a guy who could laugh like that. "I'm sorry," she said to Dark. "I'm really sorry."

Dark nodded. He put an arm around each girl and escorted them up to the porch of the ghastly Victorian house. To Marissa it was the most awful part of the whole thing: she did not want a boy's arm around her because of her nuisance value. Dark was removing them like furniture.

"This house is demented," said Violet. "This is what set me off."

Sin took the porch steps at a bound and punched both Vi and Marissa lightly in the ribs. "You guys are tough, huh?" he said, grinning. "You can handle any crunch, can't you? Teaching survival courses now, maybe, Marissa?"

Her crush on him still existed. But along with it came a desire to commit homicide. All Sin's campers began teasing right along with him.

Dark ignored the commentary. "It is spooky, Vi. This was the original summer house a hundred years ago, and the guy who built it had a thing about tree branches. The carpenter built trim out of the most twisted twigs he could find, and it does look as if the trees are growing down inside the house."

Behind them, Charles was thanking the boys for coming so quickly to the rescue, but there was nobody to rescue, and they could all go back to their sing-along. Charles said clearly to Alicia that he thought he might get rid of Vi, and Alicia said to Charles that, while the idea had some merit, nevertheless even Violet deserved a second chance.

Even Violet, thought Violet.

Marissa stomped inside without touching Vi, or looking at her. Sin kept laughing, and somehow Vi thought he was laughing more at Marissa than at Vi.

Dark said quickly, "On rainy days we play tag on this porch. It goes all the way around the house. You can circle it for hours. The kids love it."

That's camp for you, thought Marissa. Year after year there are probably boys who come back just so they can chase each other around the porch. And year after year, they're going to tell how Violet screamed loud enough to bring the whole camp down.

They were inside. The front room was enormous, with stone fireplaces big enough to stand in at either end of the room, and logs the size of canoes waiting to be burned. Only one fire had been lit. The ceiling was very high, and the furniture—well, the furniture was like nothing they had ever seen before.

"It's all made of sticks!" said Violet

Benches, tables, and even couches had been fashioned from peeled logs and bent twigs. It was rather interesting to look at, if you liked knots and whorls, but there were no cushions, and the twigs poked out like spikes.

"How are you supposed to sit down?" said Vi. She regarded her tender thighs and stayed on her feet. She had no desire to get splinter-fanny. The only cloth in the whole room was the calico hanging at the windows.

"You don't sit," explained Dark. "This is where they bring parents who have the bad manners to show up when it isn't even parents' day. They don't stay so long when they have to stand or get holes in their bodies."

Naturally Charles walked in just then, and along with being furious he was now completely offended. "My grandfather made that furniture," he said icily. "It's very fashionable now. Collector's items."

Collector's items, possibly, thought Violet. Furniture, never.

Outside the boys could be heard singing lustily to the tune of "On Top of Old Smokey."

"Sleeping in puddles is what I love best; rain on my face means a good night's rest.

Rain gets in my brain, rain gets in yours,

Our brains are diluted,

And there are no cures."

Their voices dimmed and finally vanished as they were herded back into the dining hall to finish the sing-along.

Charles muttered something about the lyrics being very suitable under the circumstances and Violet said that she had a perfectly good brain, she had just been scared and Charles said that a person with a perfectly good brain would not have—

"Now, Charles," said Alicia.

Marissa had not had much use for Alicia up till now, but she had to admit that Alicia put a stop to discussion effectively. Alicia said she had had some ideas about how to be more efficient with problems at the girls' camp and why didn't she and Charles retire for a few minutes to discuss that while Violet pulled herself together?

Personally Marissa thought Vi looked totally pulled together. It was unfair. You couldn't even tell that Vi was responsible for this whole humiliating scene. She at least ought to be staring at the floor instead of staring into Dark's eyes.

Marissa had never like Violet's kind of looks: frothy and flirty. She had figured Vi's campers would drown around her ankles while Vi scanned the horizon for cute boys.

But Vi was smarter than she looked and could

both teach Cribbies *and* scan horizons. Furthermore, where Marissa had nice funny girls, Vi had drawn all the nut cases.

Tonight, in her white pants and loose hot-pink-and-yellow-splashed shirt of cotton, sandals that were so flimsy they were barely there, and toenail polish to match her clothes, Vi looked absolutely adorable.

Impossible to imagine this Vi teaching Cribbies to float, dragging wet mattresses out into the sunshine to air, or mesmerizing twelve-year-olds with horror stories.

Charles let Alicia haul him away. "Come," said Alicia simply, as if he were a dog on a leash. It occurred to Marissa that she often spoke to her own campers like that. Come. Sit. Eat. Swim. Dive. Listen. She made a mental note to stop.

Sin sauntered over toward the fireplace without a fire and leaned against the stones, his whole posture one of a wealthy man advertising yachts, amused at the common run of mortals who sobbed over bats in their hair. Jamie walked out of the room behind him, flourishing an immense wrench. Violet thought she would like to own that wrench. It was the sort of thing that would definitely keep monsters at bay. She wouldn't mind owning Jamie, too.

"You scoundrel," Sin said to Dark. "You violent, vicious attack monster." Sin was laughing hysterically, half punching Dark and half dancing to himself, as if the room were a disco and his partner invisible.

Sin took out his sunglasses, set them very low on his aristocratic nose, looked way down at Violet, and tapped the glasses back in place. "I am count-

44

ing on you, Vi. You are going to be the source of some really good memories.''

Violet studied a chandelier. It too was made of twigs, with bulbs hanging at irregular intervals wherever the twigs notched. She was trying very hard not to cry, never having been so totally humiliated in front of so many people, but she was having a very hard run. She had never felt so alone. And Marissa—who scorned nerves and fear, who probably if she found an icy cold hand on her neck would just bite it off—said not a word in Violet's defense. Maybe I have no defense, thought Violet. Maybe I shouldn't be a counselor.

In her heart she knew she hadn't come to camp to be a counselor: she'd come to meet boys. And now she was going to pay: the boys would laugh at her and she'd spend her summer airing Laury's wet mattress.

Marissa, running out of strength, sat down, forgetting the chair design. "Ouch!" she shrieked, a pale imitation of Violet's scream, and leaped up, massaging her fanny. Sin and Jamie laughed helplessly, but Jamie took pity on Vi and Marissa and guided them to a bearskin rug on the floor in front of the unlit fire. Marissa marveled that she could have attended Camp Menunkechogue for six years and never have heard about a bearskin rug. It just went to show you how separate the girls' and boys' camps were.

Marissa sat down first. Jamie loomed over her, all muscle, all opposite sex. Back when he was just some camper, or later, dishwasher, Marissa had never even considered him a real person; just there, flicking suds at whoever passed through the kitchen.

45

Now . . . well . . . "Jamie, you look terrific," said Marissa.

"You don't have to sound so astonished," said Jamie. "I always had possibilities, you know."

Not this many, thought Marissa. "You came true all at once, didn't you?" she said.

He grinned, pleased, and she remembered that Jamie had worn braces for hundreds of years. They were off now, and the grin was cute and sexy.

How odd, thought Marissa. This is camp. My summer of joy. And what am I thinking of? Not camp.

Boys.

Oh, don't let it be spoiled for me! prayed Marissa. Let camp be just as wonderful when I'm a counselor as it was when I was a camper!

She realized suddenly that camp had been wonderful because she had had counselors who worked fourteen hours a day making it wonderful. But nobody was her counselor anymore. Nobody sat all day long making plans for her happiness, or fretting if she didn't win ribbons.

It was the most terrifying thought Marissa had ever had: from now on, she had to be her own counselor.

And the competition! Not relay races in neat lines with some grown-up making sure it was fair. But fluffy little Violets and bridallike little Alicias, who won just because they were fluffy.

Vi sat cross-legged on the bearskin rug, close to the bared yellow teeth, and Marissa, down by the tail, tucked her knees to her chin. Jamie squatted on her left, Sin dropped down to her right, and

Dark leaned against the gray stones, grinning in his strange lopsided way . . . at Vi.

Marissa turned quickly away. Was that what her night off would consist of? Getting laughed at (Vi's fault)? And getting overlooked (Vi's fault)?

"Well, Charles hates me now," said Violet gloomily.

"Charles doesn't hate you," the boys protested.

Marissa yearned to stare into Sin's eyes to see if Sin liked her the way Dark obviously liked Violet, but Sin's eyes, of course, were hidden by sunglasses. She had a traitorous thought that perhaps Sin was afraid to look at anybody without protection.

"Charles wanted me to ship all my makeup back home," Vi told them.

"All your makeup?" cried Dark, who had hauled it up the cliff to start with. "No! Never! How could he suggest such a thing! Just because this is a wilderness camp is no reason to ship home two hundred pounds of eye shadow."

Violet told Dark where he could go, and Dark, grinning, said, "Okay. Always wanted to visit there."

"What's your real name?" Violet asked.

There was a funny pause. Dark's sideways smile became a sideways twitch. Marissa had a strange sense of familiarity when she saw that, but it was impossible. She glanced at Sin, and Sin was busily folding his sunglasses up and tucking them away. He knows, thought Marissa. He knows Dark's name and it's a secret. Why on earth would it be a secret? The President doesn't have a teenage son, and if Dark were a television star I would recognize him.

47

"It's such a stupid name I don't use it," Dark said. "Have pity on me, now, and go along with Dark."

Vi began playing the king's bride in Rumpelstiltskin: "Horace?" she guessed. "Clement? Percy? Rollo?"

But Dark did not play with her. He retreated inside himself like an animal entering hibernation, and Jamie took up the conversation. "Your name is perfect for you, by the way, Violet. You have enough eye makeup on right now for camouflage in a flower garden."

Vi could feel the tears rising again. Dark wouldn't even tell her his name (an ordinary request, surely; one he must have run into at some other time in his life), and Jamie was laughing at *her*.

Alicia and Charles returned. Alicia sat on the very rim of a twig armchair and Charles remained standing. They both looked hard at Violet.

"Violet, there is a little problem you and I need to discuss," Charles said stiffly. Vi thought, Charles has decided to fire me. I can't go home. I told everybody at home I was going to meet a boy here. I told them I'd be in Maine ten weeks. I can't—

Vi's chin came up. She had a tiny chin under a generous mouth, so that, like Dark, her mouth was somewhat out of proportion. She had a sense that if she tipped her head back, gravity would keep the tears indoors, so to speak.

"I am referring to Janey's trumpet," said Charles.

Violet was completely surprised.

Janey's eight weeks of trumpet lessons had not taught her all the required notes or tone quality. (There were those who felt Janey's eight weeks of

48

lessons had not taught her *anything*.) But Janey had brought her trumpet to camp, and was waking herself up every morning fifteen minutes before reveille, and sliding alone down the pebbly path to the common room. Beating Charles to the punch each morning, Janey turned on the loudspeaker that was miked through both camps, and started to play. If you could call it playing.

Charles, hoping to outwit her, had begun moving reveille back a few minutes. Instead of 7:15, it had become 7:13, and then 7:11, and then 7:06. But Janey was always there first. It was difficult to say which hurt most—just plain getting up, which was always torture, or this year's added torture attraction, Janey's trumpet.

"Janey is very proud of her trumpet," said Vi.

"Yes, but every single morning?" said Charles. "Surely she can just play reveille on, say, Sundays."

"She can't play reveille at *all*," said Sin.

"I don't suppose anybody else brought an instrument?" said Charles yearningly. "So we could limit Janey to the first session?"

Violet said, "But Janey loves doing it. She doesn't know she's terrible. And she is managing to get up on her own, and—"

"And I want tomorrow to be her last day," ordered Charles.

Why—he's embarrassed by Janey's playing, thought Marissa. It reflects poorly on his camp image. Charles isn't on the camper's side here. Charles is on Charles's side.

Marissa hated having bad thoughts about Camp Men. She wanted Charles to be perfect. As Camp

Men was perfect. Perhaps, she thought, Camp Men is perfect only in my memory.

Violet said she didn't care what Charles wanted.

"Violet, your campers don't obey rules, you don't set a good example, you teach eyeliner application instead of swimming, and now you waltz over here and disrupt the entire boys' side of the camp by screaming like a stupid idiot, and then when you're given a second chance, you refuse to obey instructions!"

Vi crumpled. The mascara was not, after all, waterproof. Her chin tilted so far back she almost choked herself. She looked about ten. "I'm trying as hard as I can. You don't have Laury wetting the bed every night, and Claudia weeping over her parents' marriages, and Janey who has nobody to write to! And I didn't scream on purpose, I got scared! And I'm sorry I yelled like that. I was just as embarrassed as you were." Vi jumped up off the bearskin. "And Janey comes first! And if I have to escort Janey to the mike, Janey should be allowed to play reveille."

Sobbing, Violet ran across the room, yanked open the door, and fled to the Jeep.

The counselors all knew Vi was right and Charles was wrong. But the boys did not move or speak up. Marissa felt them drawing together: solid against those tears and that scene. Alicia and Charles solidified too: adults, who did not break down like that, who expected better from their employees.

On my night off! When I was going to flirt with Sin. When I was going to find out Dark's secrets and admire Jamie's body. . . . I have to be Violet's ally, thought Marissa.

Marissa stood up. She adjusted her blue-black shirt and tossed her thick hair. She felt like a horse that didn't want to take a jump. "Vi is great with the girls," Marissa defended her. Marissa swung her eyes over all of them in turn. "And you're wrong to say Janey shouldn't play, Charles."

She walked out the door after Vi.

6

---

*T*he green wilderness seemed to be wearing jewels: sparkling diamonds of lake and silver splinters of river. Violet had seen a lot of New England: Boston, Tanglewood, Newport. But this was different. This was the north woods.

There must be bear in the woods, and moose, and wildcats. Foxes and mink and bald eagles. It sounded romantic when you were looking at color pictures in *National Geographic*. But now they were actually there, in the wilderness, and Violet's cabin thought she was a leader. Violet thought, What if we get lost, the kids and I?

She hoped if that happened, she would die, which would save her having to face the parents and say, "Oh, Laury? Claudia? Janey? Uhhhhhhh—I lost them."

But of course nothing could go wrong. Charles, like all men and boys worth nothing more than the animal droppings he insisted on identifying along the trail, was nevertheless a licensed Maine guide and had followed these trails a hundred times with hundreds of girls and boys. They weren't going to have to eat raw muskrats to stay alive. Although just in case of trouble, Vi had packed eight candy bars in her backpack. It occurred to her that that was one for each girl, but not one for herself.

She liked the idea of this noble sacrifice. *Here, you have candy bars. No, I'm strong. I'll starve to death.*

She especially liked the idea of not giving Charles a chocolate bar. Charles had yelled at Vi for creating a scene the night before.

As the hike began, Charles said to Vi, "My, you're traveling light, Violet. No perfume? No nail-polish remover?"

Violet, wanting to set an example for her girls, stayed calm and peaceable and said, "We're only staying out one night."

Charles hit his chest in pretend shock. "You mean, you can last an entire night without Sweet Mauve Apple cheek color?"

It was one of the few occasions in her life that Violet regretted not being tall, strong, and muscular. She would have loved to shove Charles over a cliff somewhere.

Charles said, grimly, he just hoped Violet would restrain herself from screaming tonight. It was going to be dark, did she understand that? Could she cope with the fact that there was no electricity on Lost Loon Mountain?

If I cry, thought Violet, I'll make a fool of myself as a counselor. The girls are supposed to come to me with their problems, not the other way around! Vi fought tears. As it was, the boys thought she was a complete dope, Marissa stuck by her exclusively from camp loyalty, and Charles wished he had never hired her.

Past gray birches, through a cleft in a rising cliff of stone, over a tiny brook they hiked on. The water tickled the stony bottom and rushed away.

Laury of the wet mattresses said with dignity, "If there is any screaming in the night, Charles, it will be because we are on episode nine of the Green-Eyed Maniac. You, of course, won't know what's going on because you've missed the story. You will just be confused while we all scream."

The forest floor was carpeted with club mosses. Ground cedar, ground pine, and reindeer moss. Charles ignored Laury and lectured on. Reindeer moss, thought Violet. Tundras, arctic snow, and the aurora borealis. And if nobody else loves me, at least Laury does.

Vi shifted her backpack, trying to get comfortable. Each camper was carrying her own sleeping bag and personal things and a reasonable share of food and equipment for the hike. Vi's pack included two Bisquick boxes, the bacon, the eggs, and aluminum foil. She had never cooked outdoors but Charles was going to teach them. He insisted it would be fun. Vi thought it would be more fun if Jamie met them at the campsite with a hot meal he brought in by Jeep.

But Jamie wouldn't go out of his way for Vi again. What boy wanted to be around a girl who created scenes, or cried in front of people? Far from being Camp Girl-Meets-Boy, this was going to be Camp Girl-Loses-Boy.

Charles had assigned Janey as group leader for the morning, Laury as photographer, Claudia as journal keeper, and Missy as lunch supervisor. They had a game leader, a fire specialist, and a song leader. Nobody wanted to be cleanup chief, but when Claudia drew this assignment as well, Charles said the chief got to tell the others what to clean up but didn't have to do any cleaning up herself.

Claudia was laughing diabolically over this happy result. Nobody else was. They had barely left camp when Laury said she was out of film and needed the next roll.

"You're supposed to immortalize the hike," said Charles.

"I immortalized you yelling at Vi," said Laury.

Charles strode on ahead. Nothing that Vi's cabin did fit in with his image of what a Camp Menunkechogue leader should strive for. This hike didn't fit in with Vi's images, either. Where were the fine specimens of manhood out there rapeling down cliffs? No, she had Charles.

The hemlocks were thick, and low to the ground, so that the hikers pushed through green curtains on a trail one-girl wide. The hemlocks closed in after them, as if closing off the real world. But there was no time to get philosophical or scared. Janey was practically leading a hundred-yard dash. They trotted through the woods as if they were horses. Violet galloped over a fallen branch, cantered over a rushing brook, and took a small boulder like a fence in a paddock.

"Now, now," called Charles. "Let's not all break our ankles."

"Let's just break your ankles," muttered Vi.

Claudia giggled. "Now, Violet. Perspective, please."

"You're twelve years old," said Violet. "What do you know about perspective?"

Claudia said perspective was what her father wanted her to have when he decided to be married to Heather Anne instead of Mommy, and what Mommy wanted her to have when she decided to be married to Jonathan instead of Daddy.

"Well," said Violet comfortingly, "at least they agree on something."

Claudia stopped dead. "Violet, I hate that. If something's rotten, admit it. Don't claim that if I just had perspective I'd be happy about a double divorce. I hate people who say things like that." Claudia stomped after Janey. "I hate you, too," she flung back over her shoulder.

Charles heard this one. Violet thought she saw him smile a victory smile.

The thin frightening trail vanished, and for the next half mile they followed the remains of an old logging road. They could have been strolling in Central Park for all the character building going on. Then the blue blazes that marked the trail turned south. The hikers entered an ancient stand of pines whose branches were all dead the first fifty feet: just nasty gray stubs poking out like broken ladders. Their very own lid of green had killed them.

Vi shivered. Why am I so easily spooked? she thought miserably. Marissa wouldn't be upset by a bunch of gray, dead, reaching tree fingers.

She jumped a foot when fingers touched her cheek. "I don't really hate you," Claudia whispered.

I should have read my horoscope for the week, thought Vi, rubbing her skin to take off the horrid feeling of unexpected touch. There's probably something in it: *beware of fingers*. "I know, Claudia. Don't worry."

"I really hate *them*."

"I know."

"Do you think it's reasonable to hate them?" said Claudia anxiously.

Vi gave her a quick fierce hug. "Of course it is," said Violet, "but if you quote me I'll kill you. Counselors are supposed to be on the grown-ups' side."

"Of course I'm going to quote you," said Claudia with satisfaction. "I need a good quote for my next letter." She raced after the group.

At least she's writing, thought Violet.

A great tree, uprooted by some historic storm, lay over the trail. The girls crawled over and under it, posed for photographs on it, and rode it like a horse. *"I love to go a-wandering along the mountain track,"* they sang lustily. *"And as I go, I love to sing, my knapsack on my back."*

Laury made them pose for a photograph, but Charles made Laury get on the tree with the others so she would be in the picture.

"Val-da-ree," they screamed, "val-da-rah, my knapsack on my back. Come on, Vi, you have to be in the picture with us! Sit next to me."

"No, me!"

"No, I want to be next to Violet!"

"Charles, take lots of pictures of us with Violet."

I'm having fun, thought Violet. She began laughing, and she even made faces for Charles to immortalize. When they moved on, the trail climbed the rim of the mountain, and Vi's spirits rose with it. There was a cliff on their left, and the girls pressed against a rock face for safety, with much talk about how close death was and who deserved it most.

Vi studied the moss and the cracks in the rocks. She listened to the bird songs and smiled at the clouds. She looked down at her own sneakers, proud that she could find her footing with such mountain-goat-like certainty—

—and there by her ankles, gripping the edge of the cliff, were fingers.

7

At camp, Marissa was having lemonade with Alicia.

Nobody was sick or even sunburned and Alicia was bored. Marissa had finished a swim class, her own cabin had split for tennis and for riding, and she had a free hour.

It was such a nice feeling: an hour without responsibility.

They sat on the fence that separated the nurse's station from the camp store. It was a wooden fence, but extremely sturdy: round logs, not split rails. It was a nice height to dangle feet from.

She would have preferred a different companion, but Alicia was talking about former boyfriends, and these days Marissa was eager to hear about that kind of thing.

The Jeep drove into camp. She could tell by the sunglasses that Sin was driving. Marissa's heart jumped. He must have a free hour, too! Maybe they could spend a few minutes together. Without Violet screaming or weeping or waving a mascara wand.

"You like him, don't you?" said Alicia. They giggled like little girls. "He is adorable," agreed Alicia. "I could have a crush on him in an instant."

"Well, don't," said Marissa, and they both giggled again and hopped off the fence to go toward Sin. Jamie got out of the back of the Jeep, and Dark with him.

"My goodness," said Alicia. "Charles must have closed down the boys' side. Look at all these terrific specimens of manhood descending on us."

Sin opened the passenger door.

Alicia and Marissa strolled toward the boys. We're being very obvious, thought Marissa, wishing she had more of a reason to rush the Jeep. She got nervous at the idea of the boys watching her approach.

But they were not watching her.

They had not even seen her.

Sitting in front, enjoying the adoration, was a girl. Afterward Marissa thought it amazing that she had characterized Cathy as "a girl." For Cathy was the most beautiful girl Marissa had ever seen in her life.

She was not so much blond as golden.

She was not so much beautiful as ethereal.

Sin didn't see Marissa.

For Sin the world had vanished, voices had stopped, and memory had ceased. He was soaking in this girl the way Marissa had soaked in camp.

Beauty. Marissa did not know if she had ever seen it before in its pure form. Centerfold with a pulse.

Marissa was horrified to find she was trembling. The knowledge that she was not beautiful hit her forcefully, like the ground beneath her feet.

"Welcome to Camp Men," said Sin softly.

The girl actually gave him her hand, like a queen, so he could help her down. This was a Jeep, not a coach and four! "We were laughing so much," she answered him, "I didn't really get your name. Tell me again, and forgive me for not remembering, please?" Her voice was luxurious and rich and tempting. The boys were melting like marshmallows over a campfire.

She's a counselor! thought Marissa. How can I look at her every day? How can I look at Sin looking at her every day? I want camp to be camp, not a mating contest.

Dark and Jamie had to wait their turns to repeat their names. Sin knew it and reveled in it. Marissa wondered if Dark had told this girl his real name. She was certainly worthy of breaking secrets for.

"I'm Sin," said her crush.

"You are *what*?" The girl laughed. "I surely would have remembered that! What implications!"

"Short for Sinclair," he told her, and Marissa swore that he was blushing. "Sin."

The girl's eyebrows rose. "You actually let people call you that?" She leaned way forward as if she were going to kiss Sin. The boys laughed breathlessly. She tapped his chin very lightly with a single fingertip and leaned back again, laughing. All three boys were so close to her now, the air was probably turning foul.

Alicia looked at Marissa. "I am against it," she

61

whispered. "Doesn't the state of Maine legislate against this kind of thing?"

Marissa's hands had gotten cold. "What kind of thing?" Even her voice was no match for the girl's. Her voice was dead and dull; that voice was seductive and promising.

"Excessive looks," said Alicia. "There should be a law." Alicia marched forward to introduce herself and break up the circle of worship.

"I don't think Sin is a suitable human-being-type name," said the beautiful blond with a mischievous grin. Now her hand was resting comfortably on Sin's chest, rather in the position of a tie. Sin was looking at the hand lovingly. "I believe I'll call you Sinclair." A name that made normal boys throw up . . . and she could make it sound like a titled aristocrat. Sin shuffled his feet and blushed.

Alicia said loudly, sounding painfully nurse-y, "Good morning. I'm Alicia, the nurse. And you are . . . ?"

The boys jumped, having forgotten there were other human beings on earth. Reluctantly they backed off to let Alicia into the circle. They still had not seen Marissa.

She's reduced me to tears over Sin and I don't even know her name, thought Marissa. She could not think of a time in her life when she had literally gone unseen. It was as if the girl were so lovely that her radiance actually eclipsed anybody else. Eclipses. Primitive people believed they were signs of dreadful events to come.

"This is Cathy," said Sin reverently. "She's here to teach dance. She had to come ten days late because of important commitments."

Cathy. How deceptive a name could be. Who would suspect somebody named Cathy, just like the rest of the world, would be the most stunning girl imaginable? What on earth was she doing being a camp counselor? She should be off somewhere making X-rated videos. Auditioning for angel roles. Anything that required bodily perfection.

"And this is Marissa," said Alicia loudly.

Marissa felt like the unwanted kid at the birthday party—the one your mother makes you invite. Jamie and Sin and Dark pasted smiles on their faces for Marissa and then pivoted to give their real smiles to Cathy.

"Hello, Melissa," said Cathy. "What a pleasure to meet you."

"Marissa," she corrected.

"Melissa," repeated Cathy.

None of the boys corrected her; none of them spelled Marissa for Cathy; none of them smiled at Marissa in sympathy. They didn't care whether her name was right or wrong. She was still unnoticed. They had turned to face her, they had heard her name said aloud. But they still had not seen her.

Oh, her silly adolescent dreams of dating Sin! Exactly what she had thought they would do in the tiny remote village, she could no longer remember. But it didn't matter now. It would be Cathy with Sin.

The boys said they would show Cathy around.

Alicia said no, the boys could now return to their own camp, and she, Alicia, would take Cathy around.

The boys, with great difficulty, said good-bye to Cathy, and Cathy easily and with amusement said good-bye to them. She knew they would be back. She did not have any of the normal female fears of abandonment by boys.

The Jeep left with a flourish, the boys showing off with speed and crazy driving like the stupid lovesick adolescents they were, instead of the responsible camp counselors they ought to be. Cathy, Marissa, and Alicia stood on the grass. The heat assaulted them, in the open where it could collect and multiply. Marissa wiped her forehead. Cathy simply stood there, looking like a ray of the sun: like light and air.

The sound of the Jeep vanished.

Faintly, they could hear tennis balls bouncing in the distance. A shout of laughter came from arts and crafts. A dozen little girls burst out of the common room, and headed for the archery shack. The smell of fresh rolls baking in the kitchens filled the air. A gust of wind sent waves smacking against the empty dock.

And suddenly everything was different. Not an arena in which they jockeyed for men, but camp.

The common room, the playing field, the cabins, and the Perch returned to normalcy. An owl hooted in the woods, crickets screamed, and Marissa would have the Minnows in another ten minutes.

How wonderful it was that the boys had their side of the camp; how necessary, too, that the girls could be away from them.

Perhaps without boys around, she could make friends with Cathy. Perhaps her beauty would not overwhelm Marissa's sanity once the boys were off the scene.

Marissa looked with love at Camp Men. In minutes, the bells would ring, signaling the implacable schedule of camp life.

She yearned for it, for the containment of each activity: bells and times that gave everything a neatness real life did not include.

Camp brought satisfaction. Always little projects, little events, that began and were finished in glory.

The boys ruin it, thought Marissa. We were right when we were campers and got mad when the boys shared. We really weren't the same people. If you have to flirt and be interesting, it's fun, but you lose something essential.

Now she could remember that this was a newcomer, someone who had never seen Camp Menunkechogue, knew none of its delights, and had no girlfriends to giggle with. "Cathy, where are you from? Tell me about yourself."

Cathy tossed her blond hair. She extended her lovely legs as if exhibiting them. She made sure her T-shirt was tucked in at her slender waist. She blinked lovely lashes over emerald green eyes. Then she turned to Marissa and sighed with satisfaction. "My life?" she said, "Melissa, my life is very complicated. I hardly know where to begin, it's such a soap opera."

Alicia snorted. "I see," she said. "Your life is filled with one adventure after another?"

Cathy agreed that it was so.

"Marissa and I lead dull boring suburban lives," said Alicia.

Cathy did not seem at all surprised by this news. But instead of revealing the details of her soap opera life, she kicked off her little yellow sneakers

65

and danced across the grass to the lake to dip her toes in. "Oooooh, chilly!" she called back.

Marissa said to Alicia, "So, uh, where does Cathy sleep? Which cabin is hers?"

"Marissa dear, you must be strong," said Alicia. "Charles left instructions. I knew there would be a new counselor, but somehow I didn't think—" Alicia sighed. "Anyhow, the new counselor does not have regular counselor chores."

"What do you mean?" said Marissa. All the counselors had cabins to supervise, and drudgery to do, like kitchen duty, flag-lowering duty, and firewood patrol.

"This counselor," said Alicia, looking a little grim, "was hired only to teach dance at the scheduled times and that's all she expects to do I'm sure. This session the camp specialty was tennis and in the coming session it will be dance. And since you have one less camper than everybody else, Marissa, Cathy will stay in your cabin."

Marissa thought she might kill Charles.

Alicia said it would be a fight to the finish then, because she would be killing him first.

8

___

*V*iolet didn't scream.

Not because she was brave, but because the fingers were so terrifying that her lungs collapsed. She tried to swallow, and her throat closed. She tried to run, and her feet were paralyzed.

The fingers knotted around the edge of the cliff, scrabbling in the moss and little pebbles along the rim. The fingertips pressed down. A second hand appeared. The hands were very tan, and rather hairy. She did not believe that she had ever seen hairy hands before. Except on apes.

A head followed the hands. A head with a beard. It grinned at Vi. "Hi, there," it said. "What a great thing to find on top of a mountain."

The rest of the campers had rounded a bend in the trail. Vi was alone with the head.

"You came up the easy way," it informed her.

The head somehow vaulted over the edge, and now it was a young man, complete with torso and legs, and he turned and hauled a companion up

67

the cliff, and together they hauled a third person. All three were linked together by ropes and harnesses.

And insanity, thought Vi.

Charles's voice floated back around the mountain. "Violet! Violet!"

Her hands were dripping with perspiration. If she had been climbing the rock cliff with these guys, she would have slid back down from bodily lubrication.

"Is that your name? Violet?" said the bearded guy, grinning still, and panting. "I like that name. Perfect for you. You even look like a mountain flower."

"So," said the second climber, reaching to his side. She thought he was reaching for a weapon and flattened herself against the rocks. He brought out a canteen and drank deeply. "So. Pretty romantic place to meet a pretty girl, huh?" He waved at the spectacular view of Maine.

Vi believed in flirting. But there was a time and a place. And when your fingers introduced you, you were not Vi's kind of person. "Nice to meet you," she said. "Have a safe trip down."

And while the three mountain climbers laughed, she scurried along the trail after her girls. The laughter echoed faintly across the mountains, chasing Vi along the trail.

"What were you doing?" said Charles with a frown. "Applying mascara?"

Vi glared at him. "Just making sure I have a date for tonight," she said icily.

Charles looked as though he could not imagine Violet ever having a date for tonight. "Now, people, we're leaving the blue-blazed trail and turning north on the red. Do not get confused."

The rocks and clefts were behind them, and now, in an open scrubby mountain meadow, they found wild blueberries. The girls screamed and giggled and ran about picking the berries and smearing each other's faces blue.

Vi told them her favorite picture book story her mother used to read to her: *Blueberries for Sal*, where little Sal accidentally followed a mother bear on a Maine hill instead of her real mother.

Charles named the birds flying overhead and the two lakes they could see sparkling to the west. Then they turned, and went back into the forest: the red blazes hot round marks high up on the trees. The trail grew rockier, and the way became steeper, and anybody wearing a sweatshirt took it off and tied it around her waist. Talk stopped, and only the sound of shoes and panting was heard. Charles let a different girl lead each hour, but the original thrill of being leader was wearing off. They were too tired to follow, let alone lead.

Now they were above, but far to the side of, where the fingers had frightened Vi, and she could see the three climbers continuing up. The sheer rock face was terrifying. You could see little cracks and half-inch ledges where the climbers dug in their fingers and crampons, but you could not believe they would survive. Claudia yelled, "Hello!" as loud as she could, and one of the climbers turned to wave. "Wow," said Janey admiringly. "He didn't fall off or anything."

The red blazes were on the campers' right—and on their left was air. The great rock face of the

69

mountain just fell away, and beyond the air lay Maine, her lakes and ponds and puddles sparkling.

"A mirror broken into a thousand fragments," said Charles, quoting Thoreau.

"That's okay for you," said Claudia, "but I personally am *starving*."

She shouted the word starving, and it hung in the air, as if the mountain liked that idea—little girls starving. The campers turned it into a cheer. "Star-ving! Star-ving! Star-ving!"

Vi had underestimated Charles. He had not taken a thousand hikes with kids for nothing. They went only another quarter mile to an old fire circle. The ground was slanted here, but not enough to make Vi's palms wet with fear. The woods were thick, but with enough open space to make a fire possible. Charles gave efficient instructions, because the meal would take a long time, and hungry campers could quickly turn into crabby campers.

They built a large fire in the stone-circled pit, and as the embers appeared, they shifted them around for better cooking space.

They sliced potatoes in half, slathered them with butter, wrapped them in aluminum foil, and tucked them into the embers. They yanked down the husks from ears of corn, removed the corn silks and tossed them in the fire, slathered on more butter, tucked the husks up again, and wrapped the corn in aluminum foil, too. They gathered dead sticks to poke their hotdogs on.

"Okay," said Charles. "Now you are each to eat an orange for an appetizer. Cut the orange like this." He sliced the top third right off his orange. Very carefully he ran his penknife around the insides and gently, gently peeled his orange out, leaving an orange-peel cup and lid. "Nobody make mistakes," said Charles firmly. "I have no extra oranges."

It was very hard to get the orange out without ripping the peel. Each camper was afraid that she would be the one to mess up and ruin her orange cup. When Laury ripped hers she burst into tears. "It's okay," said Charles quickly. "It'll still work."

Violet was very aware of how tired her girls were. Laury's tears had come awfully easily. If we don't eat soon, she thought, we'll all be crying. She was irritated by the whole orange thing.

But Charles brought out of his backpack a box of yellow cake mix that required only an egg, some oil, and a little water. He had brought these in a small jar and now he had Claudia shake the jar vigorously. Laury cut the cake mix box open, leaving the mix inside its plastic bag, and Claudia dumped her liquid into the mix. Laury mixed right in the box, using the handle of a wooden spoon.

They counted out loud to four hundred strokes. "Tear aluminum squares up for everybody," Charles told Vi. But aluminum doesn't tear well. "Those aren't squares," said Claudia. "They look more like maps of South America."

"Set your orange cup in a map of South America, then," said Charles. He poured cake mix to fill each orange cup halfway. The girls put the lids on, wrapped the aluminum tightly, and lowered the orange cupcakes into the embers next to the corn on the cob.

Vi, as game leader, passed out index cards. Each card had a word on it.

71

"Once upon a time," began Vi, "there was a—" she pointed to her left at Claudia. "You have to finish the sentence using your word, and then start a new sentence for the person on your left to finish with her word."

Claudia gulped. "Once upon a time there was a *telephone pole*," she said. "But they had decided to run the lines underground and nobody needed the pole any more. It was very lonely and useless out there by the road. But then—"

"Yeeeesh," said Laury. "But then the little girl across the street got tired of wearing *blue jeans* all the time, so she held a tag sale underneath the telephone pole hoping that—"

"A *magic dragon* would need blue jeans," said Janey.

Charles said, "Time! Hot dogs on! Everybody spear your dog."

"That's sick," said Claudia. "How can you talk like that?" They crowded around the fire, Charles forcing them to cook the hot dogs all the way through, even though Claudia claimed she was going to die of starvation if she couldn't eat sooner than that.

People who had never in their lives been willing to touch a potato gulped theirs down, skin and all. People with braces who were forbidden to have corn on the cob, had corn on the cob. "I didn't eat," moaned Vi, "I inhaled."

"I love it when you're so hungry you just scarf it up," said Claudia. "That's when you know it's really food."

After that, they poked their orange cups out of the fire with their hotdog sticks, trying not to get burned. And the cups really had turned out nifty little cupcakes.

72

For a few moments the girls were quiet and content. Then Janey said, "But is that it, Charles? Isn't there anything more?"

"Why, yes, as a matter of fact there is," said Charles. "We're going to play whiffle ball in the dark, and do some singing, and then we're going to make banana boats."

Banana boats. Just like S'mores, only you could pretend they were nutritious. "I don't want banana boats," said Claudia firmly. "I want memories. I want something to happen. Bears."

They settled for banana boats, because nobody could stay awake another minute. It was a wonderful tiredness: legs that could not take another step, heads that had to lie flat or snap off. Ground cloths came out, and sleeping bags were unrolled.

Violet had just fallen asleep, it seemed, when something woke her up. It was a bad waking up: the clutching, chest-pain type, when you know something is radically, terribly wrong. Vi lay absolutely still, trying to protect herself with silence. She could hear nothing. Her sleeping bag rustled. Nothing else did. There was no moon. The fire had gone out. The campsite was entirely black.

Vi fished around for her flashlight and flicked it out over the woods, proud of herself for having such calm.

Nothing was wrong there. To satisfy herself, she flashed the light over the sleeping girls. All was well. She went back to sleep.

Vi kept jerking awake. Each time it was with the same feeling: something was radically wrong. She could not sleep. Every part of her body was jumping.

It was a primitive feeling, as if a part of her body going back a thousand generations was waking up.

Violet would have preferred to have it stay asleep. She was exhausted. Her own fear was frightening her.

And then she knew what was wrong. She was out of her bag, crossing the other sleeping bags like a dancer. Her legs were white beneath the huge pink sweatshirt she wore for a nightgown. *"Charles!"*

He was awake instantly. She grabbed his arm. "Charles! I smell smoke."

9

Violet told herself it was nice here in the wilderness. She liked being left alone on a mountainside at night with eight sleeping twelve-year-olds. "The woods are lovely, dark and deep." She quoted Robert Frost to give herself a little spine.

Well, the woods were dark, all right, and definitely deep—but they weren't lovely. Not when you were alone. Somehow or other the sleeping girls didn't make her feel less alone or less anxious.

She couldn't hear Charles anymore.

He and his flashlight had vanished into the forest. Probably been eaten by a bear, she thought. Immediately there was heavy-duty rustling in the trees at Violet's back. The bear. Hungrier than ever.

Violet whirled, looked into blackness, and decided it would be even more scary if she saw the bear. She yanked her sleeping bag over her head, then decided that was too cowardly. What kind of counselor hides from a bear? She sat up again, lasted through another rustle, and slid back into the sleeping bag.

I'm being silly. I'm making things up. I'm exaggerating.

Now Violet could hear footsteps. Not Charles. Charles wore heavy trail boots. This sound was a dreadful barefoot sort of pad. She was shivering so hard her sleeping bag whispered against her thighs. I don't have my bra on, she thought.

It seemed necessary to go to her death-by-bear with a bra on. Violet sat up, feeling down in her sleeping bag for the discarded bra—and out of the inky black, paws touched her cheek.

"Ohhhhhh," Violet whimpered, waiting for the claws.

"It's me," came a whisper. "I woke myself up, aren't you proud of me, Vi? First time this camp session."

Violet fell back against the ground, denting her head on a rock that had not been there before and gasping with relief. It was not a bear and she had not screamed. "Yes, Laury," she said, "I'm proud of you."

It did not seem the time to reprimand Laury for not going as far as the latrine Charles had made them build. That Laury had even got out of her sleeping bag was cause for rejoicing.

"I'm hungry," whispered Laury.

There was no way Violet was going to walk barefoot through the dark to where Charles had cached the rest of the food. She fished in her backpack. "Here," she said. "A reward. One Mars bar."

If she had sounded the final trumpet, she could

not have had more effect on the seven other sleeping girls. "Mars bars! Mars bars!"

They were all awake and crawling over her, demanding their Mars bars, too. The woods were full of that special slurpy chewy sound of happy people having sticky chocolate. Violet hoped Charles wouldn't choose this particular moment to return.

"Now what'll we do?" whispered Claudia. "Think of something really neatsy, Vi. Something we'll remember all our lives."

If there's a forest fire, we'll remember that all our lives, thought Vi. Of course, our lives might be a little shorter than we expected.

She said, "Gather round. I have just the thing."

Marissa had a stopwatch. Kids adored being timed. They didn't care what they were doing. Cabin cleanup or the camp song. Swimming laps or painting cardboard castles. They were always yelling, "Marissa, time us, time us!"

I ought to time the princess here, thought Marissa. See how long it takes her to snag every boy in Maine.

Marissa led Cathy up the trail. She hoped Cathy would whine about the steepness, and ask to stay elsewhere, but Cathy sprinted up as though she was used to walking on that kind of slant and said what a cute cute cute cabin it was.

It is not cute, thought Marissa. She hated that word now. Cute. It meant Cathy was laughing at the cabin. And at Marissa.

"Melissa, you have this cute little corner all for yourself!" cried Cathy. "But where am I going to fit?"

Marissa pointed to the nasty little bottom bunk in the corner that didn't have its own shelf. Everybody was storing their extra stuff all over the bare mattress.

Cathy said, "A bottom bunk? You think I'd sleep in a bottom bunk? And wake up in the night whacking my forehead on boards above me?" Cathy obviously didn't do things like that.

"I'm afraid that's all that's left."

Cathy sniffed. She said, "Charles led me to believe I would have better accommodations than this."

Marissa laughed. "He led all of us to believe that. He thinks these accommodations are perfect."

Cathy said, "I'm not even going to unpack. Charles will have to put me somewhere else. That nurse. Where does she sleep?"

"She has a bedroom in the cabin where the camp store is. There are several adults there. The cook, the—"

"Fine. I'll have a bedroom there, too. Now where is the bathroom? I really have to spruce up a little."

Marissa thought a nice little acid bath would do Cathy good. But there was no time to say this. Her seven little campers barreled into the cabin, eager to meet their new counselor.

If Marissa had been shocked by how the boys reacted to Cathy's beauty, she was doubly shocked by the reaction of her girls. Because they verbalized it. "Oh, you're so pretty!" "Look at your beautiful hair!" "Are your eyes really that color or do you have dyed contact lenses!" "I wish I could look like that when I grow up."

Cathy merely accepted this adoration as her due.

The campers introduced themselves eagerly. "Too many names," complained Cathy. "Roxanne and Meg and Emily and Heather and JoAnne? How can I possibly remember them all?"

Robin and Esther, whom she had already forgotten, hung their heads. Marissa said that she, personally, had had no problem learning all the names.

And her campers said, "It's okay, Cathy. We'll help you."

And since Charles would not be back that night to rearrange the sleeping, and when Alicia would not cooperate and turn over her private bedroom to Cathy, Cathy had to accept that she would sleep in Marissa's cabin after all. Good, thought Marissa, at least she'll have to squash into the corner and be crowded.

But JoAnne, who had the lovely top bunk by the window where the breeze came in, and the extra ledge—JoAnne, whom Cathy had already forgotten twice, said, "Cathy, I'll trade! You can have mine!"

Marissa was proud of JoAnne for being generous, but it hurt. Because it was to beauty that JoAnne was paying homage. Sheer overwhelming beauty that twelve-year-old girls saw as clearly as eighteen-year-old boys. Perhaps more clearly. Beauty Marissa would never possess.

They were all going to have crushes on Cathy. They would all want to be just like Cathy when they grew up. Cathy would say something and they'd imitate her.

And Marissa knew that one of her dreams in

going to Camp Men as a counselor was that little girls would adore her as she had once adored her own counselors.

She hurt like stabbing.

And the worst of it was, she had to go on being a counselor. She couldn't start screaming, or beat her heels on the floor, or bite Cathy's ankles, or anything. She had to pretend they were colleagues and that they liked working with each other.

"Melissa?" said Cathy. "Melissa, shall I show the girls the kind of dances we'll be learning tomorrow?"

"Please," said Marissa. "And my name is Marissa."

Cathy slid a tape into her portable cassette player and began dancing on the stage of the common room, and she danced the way a girl with her body should dance. Beautifully.

There were no boys there to see it.

But it was only a matter of time.

Marissa slid out of the common room and walked into the chilly night air to calm down.

Alicia followed her.

Nobody noticed. They were mesmerized by Cathy.

"Too bad," said Alicia, "that homicide is against the camp rules."

"I really do feel like killing her," Marissa admitted.

"Of course you do. So do I."

Marissa had never been friends with somebody Alicia's age. She wanted to ask how old Alicia was: twenty-eight? Thirty? But she didn't dare. She wanted to say, "How come you're not married?" But she didn't dare. Coming on the heels of their jealousy of Cathy, it was not good timing. But standing in the dark, sharing bad thoughts with another woman, Marissa felt okay again.

It was still camp. There were still good friends around, and sick jokes, and silly laughter, and somehow it would still be a good summer.

". . . and the temperature mysteriously began to rise. The locked room grew hotter and hotter. Gasping for breath, Gwendolyn tried to cross the room, but the brass rods of the beautiful romantic bed were too hot to touch. Gwendolyn tried to jump onto the floor, but the slick gleaming wood was starting to burn and char. The way her skin would if it got any hotter. Through the walls came the wild sick laughter of the Green-Eyed Maniac. *Getting warm, dearie?* howled the Green-Eyed Maniac. And then, the canopy of the bed began to lower."

Eight little girls clutched each other in the pitch-dark.

"Gwendolyn *screamed*!" Violet screamed, of course, for the sake of drama, and eight little girls screamed with her. Wonderful ghastly screams swallowed the little campsite in horror.

"Gwendolyn reached up to push the canopy away," whispered Violet, and the girls leaned close to catch every word. "And the canopy was solid. The lace was hiding steel. And the steel was molten hot. And outside poor Gwendolyn's horrible prison, the Green-Eyed Maniac laughed again."

They all did the laugh, just like Violet—high and crazy and evil.

Violet thought that Charles had been gone an

awfully long time. What if she had to get the girls back to Camp Men in the middle of the night? Following blue blazes in black night was impossible. Especially along the edge of that cliffside where those climbers had crawled up around her ankles. What would she do if there really was a forest fire?

"Keep going," the girls cried. "Don't stop!"

They shuddered deliciously. They didn't shudder as hard as Violet.

At least I don't have to be afraid of bears, though, thought Violet. Any right-thinking Maine bear fled during our first scream. She continued, "Gwendolyn desperately tied on pillows to protect her feet and leaped toward the window!"

"What did she tie the pillows on with?" said Laury, frowning. "I don't see how she could do that, Vi, because—"

"Shut up!" screamed Claudia, beating on Laury with her sleeping bag. "Don't listen to her, Violet, just tell how Gwendolyn gets out!"

Violet let a cruel smile play around her mouth. "And just how," she said softly, "do you know that Gwendolyn *did* get out?"

Splendid sickening screams reverberated through the woods.

Alicia and Marissa were just about to go back into the common room when a vehicle turned into the girls' camp. It was not the Jeep, nor one of the delivery vans that brought food. It was a sleek gray car. A rich parent, thought Marissa right away. Marissa hated it when parents showed up. Nobody wanted parents around camp any more than they wanted boys.

"You get rid of them," she told Alicia. "You're the grown-up."

"I hate being the grown-up," remarked Alicia. "In fact, I think for distasteful tasks like this, there should be a designated grown-up. Somebody who likes that kind of thing."

"Somebody you don't outgrow," agreed Marissa.

"Sombody like Charles," said Alicia. But Charles wasn't there, so the two of them went up to the car.

"Hi, there," said a big fleshy man sitting next to the driver. "Hi, there, young ladies. Lovely evening, isn't it?"

It was such a startling greeting. Were they lost? Had they come all this way up the private camp road for directions?

"WSZT television here," said the man, grinning hugely. His grin was remarkably like Cathy's: a person totally satisfied with himself, knowing that nobody and nothing could possibly compete with him. He was perfect, his job was perfect, his life was perfect. Marissa yearned to tell him that he was fat.

Still, if some TV station was doing a feature on Camp Menunkechogue, Marissa would love to be in it. Diving, maybe. Filmed for life. Filmed for Maine, for the world. And especially for Sin. Marissa wondered if Cathy could dive. Probably had won silver medals for it.

"Looking for young Heath Hesper," said the fleshy man, his grin staying intact even when he spoke, as if somebody else were doing the talking. It was quite unattractive.

A peculiar name. Marissa could hardly tell if it was a boy or a girl, but certainly her side of the camp had nobody named Heath Hesper, so—

"Kindly drive away," said Alicia. "You are trespassing. This is private property and the last thing we want is some pushy television crew up here. Drive on."

The man just laughed. "Now, honey, we just want to interview Heath junior a little. Find out what he's thinking right now."

"What I'm thinking right now is that you'd better leave or else I'll—"

Alicia did not in fact have any threats. She was so small she hardly rose above the roof of the car, anyway. The big fleshy man just kept grinning away at her, waiting for her to produce Heath Hesper.

Marissa was startled by Alicia's tone of voice. It was as fierce as a mother lioness. She really wanted these guys to go.

Marissa said, "You stay here, Miss Cavanaugh. I'll get the shotgun." She began striding across the field. Alicia called after her, "Get two of them. And tell the men—"

The car window went back up, pushed by an interior button (it was not the kind of car where you had to exhaust yourself rolling up the window manually), the car's soft motor purred, and it was gone. "I have to make a phone call about this," said Alicia. "You go on back into the common room, Marissa. That was brilliant, by the way."

"Phone who? About what? Who is Heath Hesper? How come I don't know?"

"Because it's a secret. Tell nobody this happened, all right? I have to phone and warn them."

There was only one secret Marissa could think of and that was Dark's. Could he really have a name like Heath Hesper? That was the kind of name that back home they called a melvin. And melvins were people with room-temperature personalities. Dark would never be a melvin! "Alicia, is Dark really Heath Hesper?" Marissa asked.

Alicia replied, "Keep his secret, Marissa. It's important to him."

She promised, but she thought, where do I know that name from? And that face? Who is Heath Hesper, anyway?

Alicia rushed to the camp office, apparently to phone the boys' side of the camp, to warn Dark, although she hadn't said anything of the kind, it was just Marissa's only guess.

She walked slowly back into the common room.

She had forgotten Cathy. Cathy had just won a hundred and fifty converts to the cause of Cathy-adoration.

Every single girl in camp wanted to sign up for Cathy's dance classes, including the painfully awkward ones who could hardly even figure out which end of a tennis racket to hold. Cathy said Charles would rearrange the entire camp schedule to do just that. If he changes the camp schedule, thought Marissa, which is *sacred*, which is *holy*, I will know that—

Could Charles be in love with Cathy? Charles was an antique, he had to be over thirty. Cathy was still in high school.

Sick, thought Marissa. But possible.

While Marissa's cabin was getting ready for bed, they wanted Cathy to go with them to the Perch and the Rain Forest; they wanted Cathy to admire the sweatshirts they slept in; they wanted Cathy to see the mail they had gotten and the cassettes they owned and the teddy bears they hugged.

They hardly remembered to tell Marissa good night.

Nine ghosts glowed in the light of one dimming flashlight.

Their occasional screams rose upward like a wolfpack gone berserk.

Violet said, "Here, Laury, just a little more Mudd and you'll be perfect. You'll find this does wonders for your complexion. Can't you feel that tightening and cleansing of a good facial mask?"

Four bodies collapsed next to them. The girls had screamed so many times they couldn't be bothered to scream again. "Oh, hello, Charles," said Laury. "Where have you been? Who are your friends?"

Four men moaned.

"Charles?" said Vi. "Was it a forest fire? I can't smell smoke anymore."

"That's because you're dead, Vi. I sent enough thoughts up here to kill a herd of moose. You're dead and you just don't know it yet." Charles glared at her. Vi flashed her almost-gone light in his face and blinked at the ferocity of his glare. "Why should I be dead?"

"Why? Why, she asks? Because I thought you were all being murdered up here, being flung off the mountain one by one, ripped from limb to limb, and we come racing up the path to save maybe one of you, if we get there in time, if we don't have cardiac arrest first, and what do we see? Nine ghosts, Violet!"

There were happy sighs around the sleeping bags. They had done it. They had a memory forever and ever. Charles thought they were ghosts. "It's Mudd, Charles," they explained. "Vi's giving us facials now that we finished the horror story. And you have to scream during a horror story. It doesn't count if you don't."

Charles just sat quietly in the dark.

"But what about the fire?" said Violet.

"It was ours," said a voice from one of the other three bodies. "You remember us. We're the mountain climbers who flirted with your ankles, Vi. We were making supper over our campfire. And we're sorry about the smoke rising up to your camp. It was perfectly safe, we promise."

"Oh," said Vi. So she had made Charles leap up in the middle of the night on a mountain in the wilderness and race through the trees by the edge of a cliff just to find a simple safe campfire. Oh, well.

The girls had scared four adults to death and had had their first facials.

Ah, camp. Memories, memories.

"We'll never fall asleep now," said Claudia joyously.

"You fall asleep now," said Charles, "or you're dead meat."

10

———

Marissa never wrote home, although she forced her campers to, but she loved to write to her best friend. Kerry's summers were boring: Kerry never did anything except sit in the air-conditioning and watch soap operas. Marissa did not know how Kerry could stand it. *Kerry* did not know how Kerry could stand it. "Another summer," she would moan. "Terminal boredom."

"Come with me to camp," Marissa would urge.

"But, Marissa, I hate the outdoors. I like a world of soft cushions and free of bugs. I like microwaved food and remote-control televisions."

At Thursday's supper line, wrote Marissa, *Violet was the letter checker. She hates writing letters herself so she lets anything pass. Claudia had a postcard her mother had left preaddressed. "Dear Mom and Jonathan," Claudia wrote and then she crossed out the Dear and the Jonathan, because, she explained, they weren't.*

That was it. That was her letter. "Great work, Claudia,"

said Violet, *"Go have some spaghetti."* Claudia gave her a kiss.

It rained. Everybody else slept through it and got soaked, but JoAnne woke up and spread everybody's raincoats over Cathy. She couldn't let Cathy get wet, oh no.

I am not jealous of Violet any more, Kerry.

Industrial-strength jealousy has entered the scene.

Wait till I describe Cathy.

Saturday night, awards were given to those campers leaving after only one session, and ribbons for teams and cabins that had won tournaments over the last two weeks. The camp was overrun with tournaments: horseback riding, Ping-Pong, nature identifications, swimming speeds, tennis— really, said Violet, it was exhausting even to contemplate.

After the final stunts and songs of the closing night of session one, the girls were tucked into their bunks and the camp counselors, representatives from both the boys' and the girls' side of the lake, all met together. "To discuss," said Charles rather grandly, "our plans and our hopes for the rest of the summer."

Marissa and Vi had plenty of plans and hopes. (Although Cathy was putting a crimp in the hopes.)

Charles listed about seven thousand new rules. Violet decided not to listen. Marissa would know them all. There was no point in two of them knowing the same things. Instead Vi studied the meeting.

Marissa had warned Vi about Cathy. "Miss Universe is with us for the duration," muttered Marissa. Suddenly Vi had seemed like a nicer person.

Violet loved beautiful things. She preferred beautiful men, but she didn't mind at all looking at beautiful sunsets, beautiful dresses, or beautiful girls. She was prepared to enjoy looking at Miss Universe.

She was not prepared, however, to watch every single male counselor also enjoy looking at Miss Universe.

Cathy had an unusual laugh. One that, in Violet's opinion, had been cultivated over many years' practice. She cooed, like a dove: a sweet chortling intimate sound.

"And I take this opportunity," said Charles happily, "to introduce a new counselor." He was practically cooing himself. "Catherine Coatsworth, our beautiful dance instructor." There was a round of applause, sweetened with a few whistles. "She'll be teaching dance and helping within a few other areas too."

Instead of being a normal person and looking modest, Cathy stood up and waved. She actually turned from side to side as if standing on a fashion model's runway, displaying each angle of her lissome body. Her little dovey coo echoed from the rafters as all the boys imitated it.

"I'm not supposed to tell this, but . . ." whispered Marissa to Violet.

Violet felt there was no finer sentence in the great English language than *I'm not supposed to tell this, but* . . . It was the *but* that was so very attractive. You just knew good things were coming. Violet leaned close to Marissa, hoping to find that Cathy was actually a dope addict unfit to be around young girls and soon to be thrown out of camp, if not the nation, in disgrace.

"I think maybe Dark's real name is Heath. A TV crew showed up on our grounds late that night when you were out camping. They wanted to interview somebody named Heath. Alicia did not deny it when I asked if Heath is Dark. I think Alicia and Charles know something about Dark we don't. And I think it's bad stuff. I think they're protecting him."

Violet had never heard anything so wonderful. Scandal, excitement, secrets? And about Dark? It was so fitting. "Wow, that's wild! Although I would prefer to hear something terrible about Cathy," said Vi.

"I'm working on it," promised Marissa.

While all the boys' eyes were fixed on beautiful Cathy, Marissa and Vi examined Dark for signs of scandal.

Dark was sitting in the back. He always sat in the back. He was not looking directly at Cathy, but had his chin down and was looking at her from under his eyebrows, the way you did when you didn't know the answer in history and you were trying to keep a low profile so the teacher wouldn't call on you, but not so low that you provoked suspicion. A TV crew? thought Vi. In the woods of Maine? By now of course, Dark *was* familiar, so it was no good trying to remember if he had seemed familiar that first day, and was really a famous star.

Why would a famous star, or for that matter a famous star's son, decide to be a counselor at Camp Menunkechogue for the summer?

Sin was trying to attract Cathy's attention. He

grinned at her, made faces at her, and used his hands demonstratively in what he probably thought was sign language to indicate he loved her.

Jamie was leaning forward toward Cathy, his chin resting on his knotted fist, his elbow on his knee. He looked exactly like Rodin's statue "The Thinker." Vi whispered, "You don't fool me, Jamie. You aren't thinking."

"Not intellectual thoughts, anyway," agreed Jamie, and he grinned at Vi.

What if every one of the boys fell in love with Cathy? What if she and Marissa were just props to keep the camp going while the boys trailed Cathy?

Vi looked back at Dark, and he was looking at her. Vi was thrilled. One person had better things to do than get a crush on Cathy, anyway! And of course had the good taste to get a crush on Vi. Dark's eyes had a faintly hooded look, like a falcon: he's drifting on winds I cannot even see, thought Vi, swept by tempests I know nothing of.

This was so poetic she had to share it with Marissa, and they both giggled at Dark. He thought they were laughing at him. He stiffened, and looked away.

"To discuss," Charles added, "our various triumphs and failures over the last two weeks."

"Is Violet going to scream again?" said one of the boys eagerly.

"No," said Charles, "but I see she's suitably made-up for the occasion."

They all turned to look at Vi. She tried to look even half as poised as Cathy did when that many people looked at *her*. Vi failed.

"Violet likes eye shadow," explained Sin to a

wondering Cathy. "And mascara, and rouge, and perfume."

Cathy smiled sweetly at Violet. "Some girls do need a lot," she said kindly. Then she cooed.

"I'm beginning to think in terms of human sacrifice," Violet said to Marissa.

"Join the club," muttered Marissa.

While Charles talked of camp philosophy ("Our motto is, *Camping is not a spectator sport*."), the boys vied with each other for opportunities to make Cathy coo.

"Campers come here to have fun, to be a success, to use their bodies, brains and eyes. I want each camper to go to bed proud of himself and herself."

Sin was sitting in the first row, eyes fastened to breathtaking bombshell Cathy against the wall. Trevor and Brandon, two other counselors, were on each side of her, but this did not stop Sin from going all cowlike over her. She's a dove, he's a cow, thought Marissa. It's practically a stable in here.

Marissa herself felt like a dishpan, or a craft-supply shelf. Just another common room artifact. But not a girl.

Charles rambled on. "Contact with the earth —sun, rain, trees, animals, insects, grass, and flowers—"

" 'Specially insects," muttered Jamie, scratching.

"Camp could be the first time a child has responsibility. He—or she—must make the bed, sweep the floor, contribute to order and cleanliness. Camp may require far more than parents do."

Violet decided to lean back on Jamie's knees. From this vantage she could be more comfortable, see

93

Dark clearly enough to wonder, and get to know Jamie's knees. He had fine kneecaps.

"Now don't forget to keep your cabin logs going," said Charles. "Remember that at the end of the summer we give out a prize for the very best. Some cabins are doing lovely illustrations, even watercolors. Try not to be the kind of people who just write down the weather."

Each cabin kept a log. Every night a different camper wrote the journal entry. Marissa remembered her own entries over the years: how the Silver team whipped the Scarlet, how her cabin saved a wounded owl, how they had once been voted the most irritating campers in Maine. "What happens to the logs?" Marissa asked.

Charles looked faintly embarrassed. "Well, Camp Men has been around for fifty-seven years. That's a lot of notebooks, week by week, cabin by cabin."

"You don't throw them away, do you?" cried Marissa. The pain in her voice was evident.

Cathy began laughing. "Melissa, what on earth would be worth saving? Fifty-seven summers' worth of complaints about supper, lists of mosquito-bite rankings, and who won the spitting contest?"

Any minute now, Marissa thought, she'll say how cute it is. And how cute I am for caring. "Marissa," she said with a great effort at staying cordial. "That is my name. Marissa."

Cathy merely raised elegant slim eyebrows. It was a facial expression she was obviously proud of, because she used it so often. "What a cute little name." Cathy smiled at Trevor, Brandon, and Sin. "Isn't it cute?" she asked them for confirmation. Yes, they said, it was cute.

"And now," said Charles, "the fun begins."

"Oh, good," said Cathy, taking Trevor and Brandon by the hand.

Charles laughed. "Not quite, Cathy. Now we are going to bid for yucky jobs."

He never laughed at me over my makeup, thought Vi. And I have kept an entire cabin happy under very trying circumstances with my makeup. But *she* coos suggestively that fun requires a pair of boys, and Charles laughs.

You were required to bid for yucky jobs. The only thing was, could you manage to bid on the least yucky job? Since Charles wasn't giving out the list ahead of time, you couldn't tell whether a job was truly the pits or whether a worse one was coming up and you should grab this one quick.

Everybody had a little bag of Cheerios, and chores were called out by number. "Chore six," yelled Charles. "Do I hear a bid for chore six?"

Violet said glumly, "I bid one hundred Cheerios."

Jamie bid one hundred and one.

"Gone," yelled Charles, "to both the eager bidders."

"You can't do that," argued Jamie. "It's either me or Violet, and it's me."

"Nope," said Charles. "Takes two to paint the latrines."

Violet and Jamie moaned, falling on the floor in humiliation and despair, while the rest of the counselors cheered loudly that they had not bid on chore number six.

"Vi?" said Sin. "*Vi* is painting latrines? But she didn't bring a latrine-painting outfit."

All the boys laughed. Violet forced a laugh, and

was rather glad she could not hear what Cathy was whispering to Brandon and Trevor.

The bidding continued, and Marissa had to caulk canoes and Sin had to replace four fence posts and Cathy . . . "You might bid on this one," Charles said to Cathy. So Cathy bid a Cheerio.

Cathy's yucky chore was counting art supplies.

Somehow all the other girls managed to look at each other all at one time. Cathy had friends in high places, but she definitely was not winning any in ordinary places.

"Time to break up!" called Charles. "Boys to the boats, please."

It sounds as if the camp is sinking, thought Marissa. And perhaps it was. Under the weight of too much Cathy.

The boys left for their camp in two groups: the ones who never noticed girls and didn't care, and the ones who whistled, pretended to sob, flirted, or shouted promises to canoe past at midnight. . . . All to Cathy.

"Well, this is it," said Sin, leaning over Cathy, clearly wanting to kiss her good night. "Now we separate for good."

This just amused Cathy. She knew nobody separated from *her* for good.

Sin whispered in Cathy's ear, and Cathy kissed him lightly, rather possessively, and cooed. "Thank you, Sinclair, dear, but I'll be going out my first night off with Trevor. How about next week?"

Sin's lovesick expression did not change at all. He wagged his body, like a dog getting a treat at the table. "That would be great, Cathy. I'll be waiting."

Sin did tell me how nice I looked that night . . . but he wasn't looking at me when he said it, Kerry! He was looking at Cathy! And when Violet corrected Cathy again on how to pronounce my name, Sin laughed with Cathy. . . . And so I have decided that Sin, like all boys, is worth nothing. Animal droppings on the nature hike are worth more.

Marissa stamped the letter and put it in the mail-bag. Kerry would write back, a letter filled with consolation, saying that nothing was terrific at home, either.

Their letters crossed in the mail.
Kerry's arrived that morning.
It was indeed reassuring.
Reassuring that Kerry, at least, had a different horizon.

Dear Marissa,

At last I don't have to envy camp! Because guess what is happening! Remember Jordan Graham, that stuck-up kid who went off to boarding school two years ago and we all hated him because he thought he was so terrific? Well, Marissa, he is so terrific. He's back in town, and I ran into him at Joanie's and he asked me out! We went to a movie. Isn't that absolutely the most boring thing you ever heard for a first date? And the movie was really sexy. I was so embarrassed sitting next to him and listening to those jokes, but he just laughed and then he asked me out for the next night, and that night we had hamburgers and went to a museum exhibit, because it was air-conditioned and the museum cafeteria has great ice cream and our mothers would feel we were getting Culture. And then the next night his uncle was going out of the city, and he took us along, and we spent the day at their house on the beach. You should see Jordan in a swimsuit. This man is perfect. And he's mine, Marissa, he's mine!

Marissa thought she could not bear it.

Deep down she had been so sure! She was pretty after all, and Sin would adore her after all, and this summer at last she would like boys *and* boys would like her. Oh, it was awful. This summer she had awakened to the fact that boys were adorable, wonderful, and necessary—and they were oblivious.

Marissa went to find Violet. Vi had unexpectedly turned into a good friend. Vi would make her feel better. They would weep together and be united against Cathy.

Marissa found Vi sitting on an old log that ran between two hemlocks down by the lake. Kids used it as a shortcut from the dining hall to swim class, pretending it was a balance beam.

Vi was not alone. She was leaning against Jamie, and Jamie was touching her cheek, and Jamie was asking when Vi's next night off was.

"Day after tomorrow," said Vi. "But it's Marissa's night out, too, Jamie."

"Aw, Marissa can take care of herself. I want us to be alone."

11

———

*H*ot and dusty.

The lake shimmered under waves of heat.

The sky was a blue so intense it seemed painted.

The scent of pines was very strong as the sap seemed to boil.

Everybody said that Maine was never like this.

Only Jamie was free to help lug trunks and sleeping bags. He moved slowly, his Camp Men T-shirt soaked with sweat. The rag tied about his forehead had to be rung out several times. He stopped constantly for lemonade.

New girls arriving for second session and their swiftly departing families probably thought he stopped for lemonade because of the heat. He did not. He stopped because Violet was pouring.

They all had their tasks, and only Marissa, cool in the lake, was happy with hers.

At first Charles had assigned Cathy to write ID tags that were pinned to everybody's T-shirts. Cathy had lovely handwriting but a less than warm welcome. "How can a person possibly remember all these names?" she said irritably to each newcomer. She grumbled about having been hired just to teach dance.

So Charles had relieved Cathy of ID-writing chores. Finally he told her there was something she could help with and he had her run the escort service to the nurse for the lice check.

"*The what*?" screamed Cathy.

Alicia said not to worry, because if anyone did have lice she would give them medication. Cathy was not reassured. "What if they give their lice to me on the way over to the nurse's station?" she shrieked.

This was a thought that sustained Marissa and Violet throughout the long day. Cathy with cooties.

Marissa was the only comfortable person in the camp. She was doing the girls' swim tests. No camper could begin anything until Marissa knew how she stood as a swimmer. People who sank had to be identified. Marissa was encouraging, complimentary, and calm—the very model of recommended camp-counselor behavior. With two little girls who refused even to touch the water, she was full of Camp Men cheer. "Yes, but if you learn to swim, a whole new world is opened up to you."

"A world of dragonflies," said one of the two girls. "Who wants that?"

"World of canoes," said Marissa seductively.

"Nasty, tippy things," remarked the second new camper.

"Waterskiing!" cried Marissa. "Speedboat racing!"

Neither girl was tempted. And a good thing, too,

since the camp didn't have waterskiing or speed-boats. Charles demanded to know what made her say that. "I figured I was safe," Marissa explained.

A ten-year-old named Dana stood outside the camp gates. "I'm still free," she mumbled. "They haven't got me yet." Dana watched everybody else getting into lines for health forms, or getting into lines for swim tests. "They're taking hostages by the score, but they don't have me. I'm tough, I—"

Her older brother dragged her unceremoniously into the enclosure. "Slave!" screamed Dana piteously. "I'm their slave now! I'll never be free!"

"No, but *I'm* free," said her brother. "I don't have to listen to you for eight more weeks." The brother began clapping his hands and dancing in a little circle as if he were trying to attract rain. Dana's brother and parents left with unseemly haste, as if afraid Dana would manage to stow away in the station wagon and they'd have her all summer after all.

Cathy strolled over to win Dana's confidence.

"I hate camp," said Dana firmly.

"But you'll be able to take dance classes with me," cooed Cathy.

"Ugh," said Dana, thus winning all female counselors forever to her case.

Parents vanished quickly. Either they were thrilled to be leaving their daughers for two weeks (or longer), or they hated good-byes.

Jamie said, "Violet, don't you have a job?"

How big and hefty and solid Jamie was! His hair matched his physique: thick, curly, and unruly. Even his speech was firm and strong. Violet had fallen in love with him when they sat on the log and confirmed that yes, he had terrific kneecaps. Now she could hardly wait to paint the latrine.

How wonderful that Jamie was so big and solid: somebody you really knew was there. Now Sin seemed skinny and pseudosophisticated, and Dark merely silly, without a real name.

Whereas Jamie was perfect.

"I am the newest escort to lice check," said Violet, with dignity. "And just what are you doing?"

Jamie grinned. "Making lewd advances to you."

"Jeepers," said Vi, "you'll have to be a lot more lewd than this if you want me to notice."

"You always notice," said Jamie.

They grinned at each other, and suddenly Vi was out of breath, and hot from her toes to her cheeks. It was impossible to look into Jamie's eyes anymore: she who never took her eyes off boys.

Too many witnesses here, Vi thought. And then wondered just what they could be witnesses to? Nothing was happening. She and Jamie were just smiling. Her own smile faded, and Jamie's faded, and both wet their lips and tried to laugh.

A ten-year-old hand tugged on Vi's T-shirt. "I'm MarMar," the child whispered nervously. "They said to go to you next."

"Your name is what?" said Vi. "You can't have a name like MarMar. What's your real name?"

"MarMar."

"I cannot call you MarMar." Violet irritably fished out MarMar's form from the envelope MarMar toted. "Marigold Marjorie O'Flaherty," she read. "You're kidding. Do your parents hate you?"

"Vi," protested Jamie, shocked.

But MarMar, of course, was thrilled to find sympathy at a camp where she had expected to find only swim tests and teasing. "I hate my full name," confessed MarMar.

"Of course you hate your name," said Violet. "Those of us named for flowers always hate our names. Unless it's Heather. To my knowledge the world's only acceptable flower name. But, no, I have to be Violet."

She walked toward lice check with MarMar and they told each other bad flower name stories.

Jamie forgot the paper cup of lemonade in his hand and it tilted slightly and poured over his sneaker. He didn't notice. A wasp noticed.

Charles said it was bad enough that Violet had given four previously well adjusted men cardiac arrest up on the mountain, but did she also have to affect Jamie's heart?

Jamie started to protest.

Then he smiled, first at the grass, then at the wasp, and finally at Charles. Still smiling, Jamie shrugged, as if to say, "That's the way it goes, Charles. Bring girls along, what do you expect?"

Little Dana refused to take a swim test and refused to learn a camp song; she refused to eat any supper, and she refused to learn the camp promise; she refused to wear a camp T-shirt, and she refused to go anyplace near the Perch.

It was with some degree of pleasure that Cathy dragged her forcibly later in the afternoon up the steep hill to Violet's cabin.

Violet said, "Oh, hi! It's Dana! You're ours! We're so glad to have you."

"Ugh," said Dana.

Cathy left, happy in the knowledge that Violet was stuck with a girl who wouldn't eat, wouldn't dress, and wouldn't even use the bathroom. That should keep Violet challenged for a while.

Dana was a pretty little girl: long, soft brown hair, freckled face, crooked teeth with braces, and a very tilted nose. "I am not staying," said Dana firmly. "I hate camp."

"Oh, good," said Claudia. "People who hate camp usually bring good junk food. Any Mallomars? Any cheese Doritos?" Claudia lost no time in examining Dana's luggage carefully.

Dana said, "I thought you had to do nature and stuff around here. That's why my parents sent me. They say I'm a television addict."

"And are you?" asked Claudia eagerly. She had never met any addicts that she knew of, television or drug, and she was thrilled that camp was introducing yet another good memory: her first addict.

"Yes. And I never watch public television," Dana added, as if hoping this news would make Violet hurl herself over the cliff. "You're apt to get trapped by a nature program. Who cares about vultures and ants?"

Nobody in the cabin spoke up on behalf of vultures and ants.

"We don't have very many vultures around here," agreed Violet. "But you know what? You've got great hair, and if there's one thing I do well, it's braid. I'd braid that hair until you looked like a Swiss goat girl."

All the girls resting quietly on their bunks turned

to look at Violet. "Why on earth," said Claudia, "would she want to look like a Swiss goat girl?"

"Well, all right, a princess. With a diamond tiara."

"You haven't got any diamond tiara," said Dana scornfully.

"I beg your pardon," Violet said frostily. "I happen to be prepared for any formal ball that might be held around the campfire." She took from one of her makeup cases a rhinestone-studded black jet headband.

When Charles appeared at the cabin, Claudia was just adding a bit of mint green to Dana's mostly blue eyelids. Wonderful complex braids danced over a glittering band.

Charles stared at the capacious makeup box, with its rows of colors and pastes and creams giving an odor of a stage dressing-room to the cabin in the firs. "Dana," he breathed in Violet's ear, "has a bit of an attitude problem. Her parents fled. Apparently Dana won't cooperate with anybody over anything."

"Funny," said Vi sweetly. "Dana looks perfectly well adjusted to me."

When Charles assigned Cathy to help with the swim tests, she didn't object.

Cathy had no sooner joined Marissa on the dock than Sin appeared on the lake, rowing a group of boys over. I might have known, thought Marissa. Just when I have a chance to show off in front of Sin, I'll be shown up instead.

The new arrivals had come in the morning for the boys' camp, and in the afternoon for the girls', in order to have less congestion on the narrow woods lane into Camp Menunkechogue. So probably this was a new set of boys already getting their first computer, riding, archery, or riflery session. Marissa had always found the yell of the archery instructor frightening. "Archers! Nock your arrows! Commence firing!" You couldn't help ducking and wondering if you were going to be pierced by a feathered arrow. Or even an unfeathered one.

Archery and riflery took place beyond Marissa and Violet's cliff, on an open area so wrapped by hillsides that you would have to make a tremendous effort to get in front of the arrows and bullets. Still, when the sound of guns exploded out over the lake, Marissa shivered.

Cathy and Marissa were the same height, and both were clad in regulation navy blue tank suits. But while Marissa was merely tan, Cathy's perfect legs were radiant and golden. While Marissa's dark hair was wet and clinging to her head, shining gold hair fluffed in layers around Cathy's lovely green eyes. And Cathy's suit draped a lovely sexy figure, the rising sun logo lying on curves Marissa would never have. Was it any wonder the boys in the large rowboat whistled?

Was it any wonder that Sin barely saw Marissa, that the boys trooped so slowly toward the trail? That Sin was not the only one to cast a longing look back—the twelve-year-olds were just as starstruck?

But Marissa did not wonder at all over Cathy's reaction. She had expected it.

Cathy smiled at Marissa. "You look so cute in your little suit," she said.

The campers dried off, changed into shorts and Camp Men T-shirts, and then neatened their cabins before supper. After the meal a very funny play was presented by a cabin whose campers had all been there for the first session and had remained for the second.

Then came the flag ceremony. Marissa loved the lowering of the flag; the special silence as it was folded into triangles; the pause, it seemed, of the whole country, while they remembered that they were Americans, and lucky lucky Camp Men girls, too.

And then Charles, softly, began the pledge.

"I promise to be a friend to people around me and to the earth,
I promise to love the world and all her glories,
I promise to encourage, to praise, and to be patient,
To let the world know—
I am a Camp Menunkechogue girl."

Cathy did not repeat the pledge. Marissa was not surprised. Cathy was hardly a girl who believed in encouragement, praise, or patience. And the only thing she loved in this world was herself.

But oh—it was so unfair—the world loved her back!

After the pledge, everybody broke quickly, each counselor rounding up her charges, heading for cabins or the Perch. Little lines of girls curled over the darkening grass.

Only Marissa noticed a new girl, lost and frightened. "MarMar, honey, which cabin are you?"

MarMar bit her lip and shook her head. She could not remember.

Marissa knelt down and snuggled her a little. "We'll find your cabin," she promised. "Cathy, would you look on the register and see where MarMar is assigned."

Cathy was irked. "I was planning to take an evening swim," she said.

Marissa felt like shooting her. The poor little camper felt bad enough without also feeling she was a nuisance. "It will still be evening when you finish looking up MarMar," said Marissa thinly.

Cathy tried to get MarMar to remember her cabin name so that Cathy would not have to cross the distance to the office. MarMar managed half a sentence, and Cathy giggled. "Where are you from, MarMar?" she said.

"I'm from the Bronx." MarMar managed a timid smile. "People are always surprised that real people really live in the Bronx. Well, here I am, a real person from the Bronx." She hopped in front of Cathy, hoping for recognition from the beautiful creature that Cathy was.

Cathy, laughing at the heavy accent, said, "I don't consider you proof that real people live in the Bronx."

Marissa was shocked. "Cathy!" She put her arms around MarMar. "Here. You and I will find your cabin together." Her voice was too loud, almost gushy. "You'll have fun tonight with all sorts of neat crazy girls in your cabin."

MarMar knew better.

She had no value in Cathy's eyes, and it followed that she had no value in anybody's. MarMar didn't care what Marissa was offering. Marissa was nobody, either.

Cathy strolled to the water's edge, peeled off her T-shirt and shorts in sensuous smooth movements, loped down the dock, and dived. She seemed to stay in midair, as if caught by a camera. When she hit the water, a wonderful wild splash rose artistically around her disappearing legs.

Violet was escorting her girls up the cliff. At the foot of the path, Jamie gave her a one-armed hug. Even from the lake Marissa could see the glow of Violet's smile.

Little MarMar wiped tears from her cheek and said quickly, "Lake water."

In all her years at Camp Men, Marissa had never shed tears, let alone needed to pretend it was lake water. This will be the year, thought Marissa, as she took MarMar's hand.

I won't make it through the summer at my own wonderful camp.

12
---

*D*ear Mariss,

Whatever is the matter? Do you realize you haven't written once in the entire second session? And this is now week one of the third session? I demand to know what is going on! You've always written twice a week. I bet you're not only leading hikes and getting bee stings, I bet that Dark or Sin or Jamie or Trevor or Brandon is in love with you. I bet Dark chose you to tell his mysteries to. I bet Sin saw through that old Cathy's glitter and shine and fell for you instead. I bet Jamie decided a frivolous little cupcake like Violet was not for him and took you out instead, huh? Am I right? Listen, Jordan and I are going up for the week to stay at his family's summer house on Cape Cod! They're going to teach me to sail! Jordan has his own car! Life is perfect, isn't it?

Love, love, love (I'm really getting into love these days).

Kerry

UNDEAR MOTHER AND FUTURE STEP-
FATHER—

I AM BEING FORCED TO WRITE THIS LETTER.
OTHER THAN LETTER-WRITING CAMP IS QUITE
QUITE NICE. WAIT TILL YOU SEE HOW WELL
YOUR DAUGHTER CAN APPLY MASCARA, EYE
SHADOW, AND EYELINER. WHEN I AM A
BRIDESMAID FOR YOUR SECOND WEDDING
(WHICH NO TRULY DECENT PARENT WOULD
HAVE ANYWAY), MY FACE WILL BE SPECTAC-
ULAR. I HAVE GAINED 200 POUNDS SO WILL
LOOK ESPECIALLY ATTRACTIVE IN THAT PUR-
PLE GOWN YOU WENT AND BOUGHT WITH-
OUT ASKING IF I LIKE PURPLE. HAVE
DEVELOPED A SERIOUS MOSQUITO BITE AL-
LERGY AND MAY WELL DIE BEFORE THE WED-
DING ANYHOW. IN THAT CASE, YOU MAY
HAVE MY PAINTED ROCK COLLECTION TO
THROW AT EACH OTHER.
HATEFULLY YOURS, CLAUDIA

"Claudia, you can't mail that."

"Why not? Are you going to censor my personal
letters, Violet? That is un-American. I won't put up
with it. I know my constitutional rights."

"Nobody has rights in a camp. Here's a fresh
piece of paper. I'll dictate and you write. *Dear Mommy
and Jon*—"

"If I vomit all over your feet, and we lose cabin
inspection again, it's your own fault, Violet."

"You vomit all over my feet and you can lick it
up, Claudia. Dana, what are you laughing at? Dana,

stop laughing. Dana! Did you use up the last of my Sheer Violence perfume? You creep, Dana! Claudia, write your letter! Janey, stop drumming your feet against the bunk on top of you! Somebody turn off that radio! I hate that station! Claudia, do not stick your fingers down your throat."

Dear Mother,

Camp is more fun than I thought it would be. Can I stay another session? Violet is so much fun. The best time is rest hour when we drive her crazy. I'm not as good as Claudia, but I'm getting better every day. Charles inspected yesterday and we lost again. Violet threatened to throw Charles off the cliff. We had to hold Violet down.

"We're talking a log cabin here," Claudia reminded her. "And whether or not the sneakers are lined up in little rows under the bunks. We are not talking high treason or the end of the world as we know it."

"Camp is going to my head," Violet muttered.

"It already went," said Janey.

Listen, for my birthday can I have some Sheer Violence perfume? The perfume you could kill for.

Love, Dana

Dear Mom and Pop and Todd,

I am having such a good summer. Especially wait till you hear me play my trumpet now! One of the boy counselors is giving me trumpet lessons. His name is Dark. All the girl counselors think he's cute. I guess he is. All the girl counselors like to grade the boys, and nobody gives him less than A-minus. I am learning how to grade the boys. All the boys my age are F's. We have to be with them sometimes and that stinks. They stink. They're even lower than F. In fact I am quitting computers because of all these boys in it. Yucky. Anyway, I now play the best reveille you ever heard in your life. Dark taught me. I think maybe next summer I'll bring lipstick and stuff and go out with Dark.

Love, Janey

Dear Grandmother,

Thank you for the generous check you sent for my birthday. I have a girlfriend now, although she is trapped by being a camp counselor, which cramps my style taking her out. Anyway, you would like her. I bet you looked like Vi when you were sixteen. I want you to know that, in accordance with your instructions, I am not saving for college, I am not contributing to my car insurance, and I am not buying anything sensible. I am taking Violet out. (Mom and Dad do not approve, Gram. They say you are frivolous. They say Vi is pretty frivolous, too.) I will keep you posted, Gram, but I may leave out some of the details.

Love,
Your grandson, Jamie

Dear Sis,

Honestly, life can be so lousy.
I was feeling so good when I got here: in control of my life and all that kind of thing. Now the guy I love is flirting with the most beautiful girl on earth. I can't hold a candle to her. You think I exaggerate?

Cathy takes away my breath and I reserve breathless-ness for men.

This girl is so accustomed to adoration that she is entirely selfish. It's rather frightening.

Her best skill is laughing at other girls. She laughs at the campers, and she laughs at the counselors. She has a horrid knack for making other people join in the laughter, so that the victim is publicly humiliated.

And not only am I jealous of Cathy, I'm jealous of Violet!

Violet attracted this hunk named Jamie. Jamie looks like Daniel Boone, and when he flexes his muscles the little boys all want to grow up to look just like him and the older girls all swoon. Jamie's very sophisticated, but the campers think only hicks know how to do things like cut down a tree: therefore Jamie's a hick. Jamie loves this. Let the other boys strive to be sophisticated; Jamie strives to be a woodsman. He is a great big guy and Violet is tiny and they make this adorable couple, although all the tall girls are furious that as usual the only guy tall enough for them is dating a miniature.

Cathy has decided to ruin Violet. Jamie fell for Violet just as Cathy walked in the door, which is visible proof that Cathy can't win them all. Cathy's going to get Jamie if it kills her. (We all hope it does.)

Love, Alicia

Dear Mommy and Daddy and Mark and Sarah and Courtney,

I especially wanted to be in Marissa's cabin this summer and I got it, but now I'm sorry. Violet's cabin has all the fun. Marissa just hangs around and mopes. She depresses me. Like nature. We have to do leaves and animal tracks and barometers. Violet's cabin is always doing something fun. Yesterday they made an ice-cream pizza. You spread vanilla ice cream in the pizza pan, dollop it with strawberry ice cream for the tomato sauce, and use little chunks of chocolate for pepperoni. Would you write and see if they could transfer me into Violet's cabin?

Love, Roxanne

Dear Mom,

How are you bearing up?

It's nice not to have to deal with it, but I feel bad leaving you there. It's on my mind all the time, and I have a hard time focusing on my job and on the kids. Luckily I have a very demanding cabin of little boys and I keep giving myself other chores, since I can't sleep anyhow. Now I'm giving music lessons at dawn. Also, I'm thinking of asking a girl out for no reason except to keep me occupied on my days off. Not very romantic, is it?

Listen, hang in there. If you really can't last any longer, I do recommend the wilds of Maine. There is a certain peace here. Of course, that also just gives more time in which to realize what is happening to us.

Love, Heath

Dear Mom,

I am so in love! I just knew it would happen this summer, I knew it when I packed my hot rollers. Wait till you meet Jamie. Oh, he is so perfect. Of course we've only had one real date because my days off don't come very often, but we drove to his favorite lake. It was no different from our own lake that I could tell, but Jamie

115

thought it was more perfect. All Maine lakes are perfect, you see, but your own Maine lake is the most perfect.

Speaking of perfect, Jamie is, too.

I hate Cathy just as passionately as I love Jamie. Now if I don't get around to killing Cathy, I'll probably kill Charles instead. (I had no idea that camp would be so emotional.)

Today Claudia got letters from her stepfather-to-be and her stepmother-to-be and so I have to keep her from killing them.

(Actually, I am exaggerating here a little. I don't want you to think we sit around sharpening knives. Although Claudia does think we should all take archery and riflery next session just in case.)

> *Love, Vi*

My Dear Mr. Crandall:

Of course Roxanne is happy this summer and has always been happy at your fine Camp Menunkechogue, but she seems to be having something of a personality conflict with Marissa. Kindly move her into Violet's cabin.

> *Sincerely yours,*
> *Veronica Chaplin (Roxanne's mother)*

Dear Claudia:

Thank you for your sweet letter. I'm so glad you're feeling better toward us.

Wasn't it just so sweet of my darling Jonathan (and of course also of Heather Anne) to write to you at camp!

Your bridesmaid's dress is an ivory lace overlay on a deep plum gown, very rich-looking, and very frothy! What a wonderful change after ten weeks of Camp Men T-shirts, huh?!!!?!

Mommy is enclosing a fascinating clipping. Did you know one of your counselors up there is the son of a very famous crook? The father is being investigated even now, for multimillion-dollar-Wall-Street rip-offs. Apparently he's stashing his children in out-of-the-way places like Camp Menunkechogue while he's testifying before the grand jury. I hope the man gets 20 years in prison, he certainly deserves it.

Have fun! See you in six weeks!

Love, Mommy

13

---

*H*er day off was the lowest point in Marissa's life.

She had not been able to admit to anybody that she even had a day off, although of course the schedules were posted, and any counselor who cared could check.

But no counselor cared.

The day loomed like a mountain in front of her: all those sixty-minute hours with absolutely nothing to do. And more importantly, nobody to do it with.

She had never been unloved before. What a thing to learn at camp! How to survive friendlessness.

She spent every day shoring up children: buttressing them against any problems, being sure they ended each day in triumph. And she had enough control over their lives at camp so that she could indeed arrange this.

Perhaps you had to be twelve or under in order

to have somebody arrange happiness for you. Perhaps once you got older, you could not arrange happiness: you just had to endure and hope that it came on its own. Or else locate somebody who would want to take up your happiness as a cause. Violet had. Jamie shirked none of his tasks: the grass was mowed, the hemlock hedge trimmed, the cabin steps repaired, the broken downspout replaced. And yet Jamie always seemed to be near Violet. Jamie did such neat things: like that ice-cream pizza he set up for Vi's cabin, so that immediately every other cabin had to do it, too, or die of ice cream deprivation.

Marissa would never forget Charles quietly asking her to come to his cabin. He asked her to sit down in the chair across from his desk. She thought from Charles's heavy, sad expression that perhaps somebody in her family was dead. Then he showed her the letter in which Roxanne's mother asked for her daughter to be switched into Violet's cabin.

"Now you and I know that nine-tenths of what the campers write home is made up," said Charles, "but this must have sprung from something."

Marissa just burst into tears.

"I guess you are a little depressed," said Charles. "Do you want to tell me about it? I'm here to help. I want the camp to run smoothly. Whatever it takes."

He was like the rest. It didn't occur to Charles to worry about Marissa herself. He just wanted the girls in her cabin to be happy.

"Listen, I'm going to give you an extra day off. You cheer yourself up, and then I'm sure everything will be fine."

An extra day off.

Marissa could think of nothing less likely to cheer her up.

And now it was hard to be there with Roxanne at all: to know that Roxanne had committed the ultimate betrayal of asking her parents to put her in somebody else's cabin.

It's not my fault Violet is such a ding-a-ling! It's not my fault all her cabin is ding-a-ling with her and it makes them look special! It's not my fault that I'm good at basics, like canoes and swimming and hikes, and Violet is good at unusual things! It's not my fault that Cathy is so beautiful and I feel so plain and useless next to her.

Marissa hardly even slept the night before her extra day off, lying there in her bunk wondering what she would do all day. She could not stay in camp. She would just weep, watching other people be better counselors. But even if this were New York City, Marissa would have a hard time. She wouldn't want to go to a single department store or museum alone and friendless. And this was Maine. There was nothing out there but more trees and more lakes and more teeny towns you drove through so fast you always said, "This is a nice village we're going through, wasn't it?"

In the morning, Cathy did row movement with Marissa's cabin.

The girls stood in a long, slightly curved row, so they could all see each other, and one after the other they repeated a motion, so that the movement rolled down the line. They windmilled their arms, then did high kicks. They went faster and faster, timing

120

their movements so the result was like a wave on the ocean.

At first Marissa thought it was wonderful, and she had to add to her basic jealousy of Cathy a jealousy that Cathy was such a good instructor with awkward little girls.

Then she realized that Cathy's assignments were getting harder and harder; that girls with no dance or gymnastics background were not going to be able to keep up.

Cathy began calling out, "Okay, Meg, sit down. Emily, sit down. Esther, sit down." Cathy made the dance one step more complex and giggled at the girls' attempts. "JoAnne, give it up!"

By now four of the eight had been taken out, and Cathy turned the lesson into an elimination contest. Half cheering, half jeering, Cathy added a little skip in the middle of an already difficult step, and Roxanne couldn't do it.

"Roxanne," said Cathy, laughing. "And I thought you were good."

Roxanne turned red, and sat down quickly, staring at the knees she drew up to her chest to hide her humiliation.

"Okay," said Cathy. "We'll divide for the rest of the class. The good ones here, the crummy ones there."

Even though it was Roxanne who had asked for the cabin transfer, Marissa could not bear it. "Cathy, you can't talk like that!"

"Why on earth not? That's what you do in swimming. You divide them into Dolphins, Minnows, and Cribbies."

"But—but we're not mean," said Marissa.

Cathy cooed. The sound singled Marissa out, and made her an interfering fool. The campers tried not to look at Marissa.

Cathy said, "I thought this was your day off. Don't you have anything to do? Don't you have anybody to do it with!"

Marissa fled.

On this particular day there were two major outings: many of the boys were off for a rock hunt, where they went to abandoned mines to dig (under supervision) for precious gems. A large group of girls was driving thirty miles to take a ski lift up a mountain, with a hike back down. All the camp vehicles were in use and she could not have the Jeep, anyway, since she didn't have a driver's license yet.

Marissa felt like hiding in the Rain Forest all day.

She forced herself to go into the kitchens. The cooks made her a backpack lunch and snack, filled her canteen, tossed in two little cardboard boxes of lemonade, and Marissa took off for a forest hike.

She chose the yellow-blazed trail because it was a grade B hike: difficult terrain and some poor footing. She wanted a trail that would force her to pay attention.

Nobody yelled good-bye to her, nobody asked where she was going, nobody said, "Can I come, too?"

She almost ran the first two miles. Putting Camp Menunkechogue behind her was essential. She went over rocks, tree roots, swamp, and pine needles; through forest and between boulders; in dark shaded woods and open meadows. By noon, Marissa was more calm. She had walked off a lot of her despair. She sat down to eat.

It occurred to her that she had made no real provisions for this hike. In all her camp training she had had buddies. Safety rules required care: when you took your girls, you had to have water, and first aid kits, and leave your route with Charles, and take jackets no matter how hot it seemed, and remember compass, flashlight, insect repellent, and even toilet paper.

Marissa had brought nothing but lunch and lemonade.

She had even forgotten her watch.

The sun went behind clouds.

For a moment she was chilled.

She started to eat a potato chip, but something in the forest crunched first.

For a moment she was afraid.

She flexed her toes, and that tiny movement was enough to break the fraying lace on her left sneaker.

She thought, I'm not very well prepared for this hike.

The sun stayed behind the clouds.

With half its campers gone on all-day trips, Camp Menunkechogue had a strange temporary feel—as if today wasn't really camp at all, merely a substitute. There was not enough noise, not enough action. People were slightly nervous without knowing why.

One of the older cabins would be leaving in the morning for a three-day canoe trip. They had taken their tippy-canoe test: each pair of girls had to go out in the middle of the lake, tip the canoe over, and right it. Then their counselor, sitting in the rowboat, made them swim to shore. This was to establish physical fitness. What it actually established was *lack* of physical fitness.

"Alicia!" the girls yelled when they staggered onto the sand. "We need massages!"

"Your camp nurse doesn't do massages."

They grumbled. What good was she?

Dark's computer class was designing a program for star patterns in the sky above Maine in July. One girl ignored this less-than-thrilling assignment to design a letter home: seventeen printed pages of the same words solidly repeated: CAMP MOS-QUITO, CAMP MOSQUITO, CAMP MOSQUITO. When her group reported for swimming, she hung her seventeen page message on the towel line.

"Really," said Alicia a little huffily, "they aren't that bad this year."

"Are too," everybody clamored.

"Our cabin had a contest to see who had the most mosquito bites and I didn't even win," said Claudia, displaying legs and arms that were prac-tically measled. Alicia might have known Vi's cabin would have a mosquito-bite contest. "What we get for going near the woods," muttered Claudia.

Alicia said she thought a more cheerful attitude on Claudia's part would make the woods more ex-citing for her, that you just never knew when you might see a deer or a fox.

Claudia said could Alicia please not be so cheer-ful. It was annoying. When every inch of your body itched, cheerful people were not good company. Only screaming itchy people were desirable.

124

Vi had no Cribbies left: they had all advanced to Minnow.

She sat on her towel and applied toenail polish while Cathy helped with the tippy-canoe tests. Vi was not surprised when Sin suddenly found that his cabin also needed to do tippy-canoe tests. Suddenly, the middle of the lake became coed.

Dark brought his computer boys to the end of the dock. "Nice toes, Vi," he complimented her. "Hey! Sin!" he shouted. "Get the boat over here and take these kids back!"

And so it was that for a few minutes Sin and Dark and Cathy and Vi and Alicia were all on the end of the dock together.

"You know," remarked Cathy, shaking water off herself, a wonderful chance to draw yet more attention to her beautiful body, "I don't believe I've ever seen you in the water, Vi."

"I don't do water," said Vi.

"I thought all counselors were required to swim," said Cathy. "You mean you're a non-swimmer?"

Vi said, "We thought all counselors were required to take a cabin, Cathy. You mean you're a non-counselor?"

Dark grinned.

Vi's girls gathered around.

Cathy lined up the girls near her and said tauntingly, "Let's make Vi do a tippy-canoe test."

"Now wait a minute," said Vi.

Claudia and Janey sprang forward to defend Violet. "Vi is a brilliant swimmer, aren't you, Vi?" said Claudia fiercely.

"Certainly. But my toenail polish isn't dry. Ask me tomorrow."

125

Cathy implied that Vi's honor was at stake, and with it the honor of her cabin. She managed to make the twelves feel that if Vi could not succeed at tippy-canoe, then Vi was hardly worth calling a counselor.

Dark said, "Cathy, relax, huh? Back off?"

"Why, Dark, darling, perhaps I should tell them your sad sordid little history," said Cathy very quietly. She beamed at him publicly and linked arms with Sin. Sin looked confused by Cathy's remark, but Vi knew what it meant. She had read Claudia's mother's note. Well, she could not let Cathy open up poor Dark's can of worms.

Vi lifted her chin and said in a trembly voice, "I can tippy canoe. I can tippy canoe just fine."

Cathy laughed.

Vi's girls did not. They had never seen Violet tremble. What they saw now was not reassuring. Vi could hardly even get into the canoe, let alone figure out how to paddle it. As Vi made her feeble way out into the lake, Dark called out, "That's far enough, Vi, don't go out in the middle."

But Cathy said, "Dark, she can stand up on the bottom where she is now! She has to go out in the middle."

Dark felt a little hand in his, and looked down. Janey, terrified, was gripping his hand.

He was an excellent swimmer. He could easily swim out to Vi if she got into trouble. He thought, I've got to stop this *before* she gets into trouble. I really don't think she can swim. I've never seen her in the water. "Janey," he whispered, "can Vi swim or not?"

Janey turned scared eyes on him. "I don't think so."

Dark yanked another canoe up close and started to get in it to paddle after Vi.

Cathy giggled. "Oh, that's sweet, Dark. I love it. Dark the hero. Dark the rescuer. Dark the life-saver."

Vi's tippy canoe came faster and less gracefully than anybody expected. She didn't expect it, either, and yelped foolishly, hitting the water in a belly flop. The canoe tilted, and Violet sank.

The canoe did not right itself, but lay on its side, filling with lake water.

Violet did not surface.

The half-empty camp stood quiet under the hot sun.

The lake water remained undisturbed.

Claudia, Janey, Laury, and Dana began screaming in horror.

14

*E*ven Cathy was not accustomed to murdering counselors.

She dove off the end of the dock. Sin hit the water moments later. With powerful strokes they headed for the canoe. Dark's canoe shot ahead of them.

The little girls on shore screamed in terror and excitement. The older campers went into the water, too, evidently figuring the more lifesavers the better.

Cathy dove beneath the water by the sinking canoe, and surfaced in a moment screaming, "I can't find her, I can't find her!" Sin went under, and came up alone. They alternated, diving, surfacing, and screaming.

Dark simply sat in his canoe.

Alicia, her arms around most of Vi's cabin, whispered, "That is sick. That boy is heartless. Look at him just sitting there."

After a bit Dark paddled back toward the dock.

Alicia could not believe it! And she had protected this wretched excuse for a human being from prying television!

Claudia snickered.

Janey put a hand over her mouth.

Laury squatted on the edge of the dock and gave Vi a hand up.

Dark was grinning from ear to ear. Vi had been fine all along. She had swum way underwater and had surfaced on the far side of Dark's canoe, not even out of breath. When Dark paddled in she just swam alongside.

Out in the water, Cathy and Sin kept screaming and diving.

Charles came racing over the grass, racing over the sand, racing down the dock, practically plowing through Vi's campers and all but knocking Alicia into the water. "What's wrong, what's wrong?" he shouted.

Cathy, treading water, screamed, "Violet has drowned!"

Charles looked at Violet standing next to him.

She smiled sweetly.

"Are you drowning?" said Charles.

"They think so. Isn't that good enough for you?" said Vi calmly, taking Janey's towel. She looked down at her feet. "My toenail polish is ruined. And my hair is straight. If I've said it once I've said it a thousand times: Life with straight hair is hardly worth living. Somebody get my hot rollers plugged in."

Charles said in a carrying voice, "Sin! Cathy! She's right here! Swim back to the dock."

Afterward Vi told Marissa it had been worth the

129

whole summer to have sixteen campers laughing at Cathy. "Such a warm delicious feeling," reported Vi. "And I missed it," mourned Marissa. "Maybe it'll happen again," said Vi hopefully. But they didn't really think so. It was too much to hope for.

Since Vi had not drowned, Cathy tried to kill her when she reached the dock. "You swam underwater!" screamed Cathy. "You swam over behind Dark's canoe and paddled alongside it back to the dock! You let me think you couldn't swim."

"I did nothing of the kind," said Violet. "You jumped to that conclusion. I don't go underwater because I'm afraid my contact lenses will swim off without me, and I refuse to get my hair wet. If it makes you feel better, I consider that wet hair in public is practically as bad as drowning altogether."

Charles muttered, "You are such a troublemaker!"

But it was difficult to tell whether he was referring to Violet or to Cathy.

It was, incredibly, only lunchtime.

Claudia could not believe that such an action-packed day was taking such a long time. Not one girl in the cabin got any mail. They seemed to have run out of things to talk about, and the half-filled dining hall was quiet. Only the sound of chewing and swallowing could be heard.

Violet said, "Now, we're going to be doing a play based on *Little House on the Prairie*, because we're responsible along with Marissa's cabin for next Friday's entertainment. *Little House* is nice because it'll take six of us just to be Ma and Pa and Mary and Laura and so fourth."

Claudia knew the *Little House* books by heart.

The only one she didn't like was *The Long Winter*, where the Ingallses practically starved. It was too scary. Even the book was too long, just like the dreadful winter.

But where Charles and Caroline stuck together and adored each other through everything, oh, those books were so wonderful! Her favorite chapter was where the cow stuck its foot through the roof of the underground house and Ma said, "Oh, Charles," which was all she ever said, even at her maddest.

Claudia thought of some of the things *her* parents had said at their maddest. Could she do *Little House*? She would cry, wishing for the Ma and Pa she did not have, and was not going to have.

Claudia got up and pretended she had to go to the Perch.

She wished Marissa were there. Marissa had been sad lately. Marissa knew how it felt to be sad. Violet was too bouncy. Claudia thought she might go find Marissa and they would cry together and feel better.

Jamie said to Dark, "How come you didn't tell me this sideshow was going to happen so I could come watch? I feel deprived."

"I didn't know," protested Dark. "I was going out there to save her, too. She's quite an actress. The trembling chin, the awkward paddle, the whole thing was brilliant. It was just that as I got out there, she surfaced on my side with a finger on her lips for silence."

"I'm crazy about her," Jamie said.

Dark smiled. He wasn't crazy about anyone right now. He had had all the stuffing taken out of him over the last horrible six months at home. And Cathy's hissed threat had made him physically ill.

No way he could eat lunch.

"Listen, Jamie. I don't have any computer classes this afternoon and my own cabin went on the rock hunt. Any chance I could borrow your motorcycle and get out for a while?"

"Hey, sure. Good idea. You know a really neat place to go? The power lines. That cut in the woods makes a fantastic bike trail. You're all alone, but you sure can't get lost."

Head tucked inside Jamie's helmet, knees gripping the cycle, hands tight on the bars, Dark was blessedly mindless. He was soaked in the noise and the pulse of the cycle.

So Cathy knew.

They must all know.

Out of the camp, he ceased to be Dark. He became Heath again: rich kid of a rich man. A man who, it turned out, had gotten rich manipulating other people's money and keeping whatever he felt like. Even now, what hurt Heath most was not the scandal, not the pressure of the media, not the courtroom, but the fact that it was true.

My father is a thief. My father maintained our

whole life—from the prep school to the Ferrari, from the country house to the ski lodge, from the Christmases in Paris to the jewels my mother wore —by stealing.

His mother—who loved their life; loved every jet-set, million-dollar moment—had been so shocked she had abandoned it. Nobody knew that the luxury penthouse was empty, and his mother and his little sister were living in a small dull apartment that his mother could afford on her own income. Both Heath and his mother suffered permanent nausea that never quite left, ruining every meal, destroying every night's sleep.

The only thing that kept Heath going was work. His campers were at an age to worship him. Little did they know what they were worshiping. But from the glowing postcards his little boys wrote home (Heath was tougher than Violet; he required a minimum of three sentences, whereas Vi settled for a single word), he had certainly satisfied his boys.

And there were other triumphs; Janey could actually play reveille now, thanks to him.

Laury, who took computer with him had broken down and told him through her tears of shame that she had a nighttime problem and he had given her his wristwatch, which had a tiny alarm, and his good pocket flashlight, and now Laury was getting through the night.

And it was good to be around good people: he liked Trevor and Brandon; Jamie was a great guy, and Sin had been fine till he fell in love with Cathy. Alicia was a solid sensible-type nurse, and Charles a solid sensible-type camp owner. Marissa was quieter than his first analysis, and Violet crazier.

Cathy, of course, bore a certain resemblance to Heath's own father, with her tremendous ego. Anything was fine if it suited Cathy's purpose.

Sometimes when they repeated the camp pledge at flag lowering, Heath wondered about people like Cathy and his father. What were they thinking of when they mentioned honor, or loyalty, or goodness? Did they have a different definition? Or no definition?

Or did they think such expressions comical?

Heath went down the power lines.

A swath about thirty feet wide sliced through the thick woods, and the great ugly gleaming towers held wires far overhead. A whole new type of vegetation sprang up where the forest had been cleared, and Heath kept scaring deer browsing by the pylons.

Summer was half over, and he was halfway to having to go back and face the media with his mother.

Heath rode fiercely and dangerously, concentrating every molecule of his abilities into the ride. He bounced off rocks, and leaped over low spots, and roared between scrubby blueberry bushes.

Marissa was exhausted.

She normally walked this far without a blink of an eye, let alone a blister on the foot, but depression is very tiring. Nervousness about her poor planning did not help.

The yellow blazes emerged into a wide, open

space so suddenly that it was eerie. She blinked in the sun. Huge utility structures were like creatures from Mars, solidified in an alien atmosphere.

She reached for another lemonade packet, but she had drunk them both. She unscrewed the cap of her canteen, and found the water was hot.

Marissa began to cry.

She could never have cried at camp. Let her campers see her? Never. Let Cathy see her? Worse. Look what happened when Charles saw.

But here, she could weep.

Marissa felt that she was weeping for her entire life: for hopes that would never come true, boys who would never love her back, triumphs she had lost, and friends she had not made. And the worst despair of all: that she was not, and never could be, beautiful.

A helicopter roared overhead and she looked up, her tear streaks gleaming in the sun. But she couldn't see the plane. It roared louder, frighteningly, and suddenly there was so much noise it drowned her. Too late to flee into the forest, she saw a motorcycle bearing down on her.

In the camp's tiny nature museum was a tiny door with a tiny sign:

Behind this door
is the most dangerous animal in the forest.
Open carefully.

When Marissa had first come to Camp Men, at age nine, she was afraid to open the door. How could the camp keep the most dangerous animal right there in the closet to attack little campers?

135

With her buddy, she gathered enough courage one day to open the door.

Inside was a mirror.

The most dangerous animal in the forest was man.

Marissa looked at the black-clad motorcyclist, and thought of drugs and random violence and rape, and she jumped up, trying to find a yellow blaze, trying to vanish in the thick woods where no motorcycle could go.

15

*I*t was with reverence that Marissa's girls gathered in their cabin that night. *Their* counselor had come roaring back into camp on a motorcycle. *Their* counselor had had a black helmet on, and her arms wrapped around Dark's waist. *Their* counselor was more special than anybody else's counselor.

"All of it," demanded Roxanne.

"Leave nothing out," ordered JoAnne.

"Remember in court you have to tell the truth, the whole truth, and nothing but the truth," added Esther. "Think of us as your jury."

Marissa just smiled and said nothing.

"Marissa! You have to talk! Details! Is he in love with you? What did you do? What are you going to do next time?" they screamed.

Marissa just smiled and said nothing.

"Look at that smile," said Roxanne. "If I have ever seen a smile hiding big secrets, it's that one."

"Just give us a hint," they begged. "Is it a big secret? An important secret?"

"A *romantic* secret?" they whispered.

But Marissa just smiled and said nothing.

Field day was just one crazy competition after another.

Marissa was in charge of the grass races: they had three-legged races and egg-on-a-spoon races, they had twenty-yard cartwheel dashes and bite-the-apple relays. Everybody loved bite-the-apple. You had to carry the big red apple in your teeth, race one hundred feet to your opposite team member, and she had to bite the apple out of your mouth and run back to the other end. It was a pretty ooky apple by the time the relay was over.

Half the cabins were Scarlet and the other half were Gold. Marissa and Violet's cabins were both Scarlet, and the two counselors screamed themselves dizzy and hoarse for Scarlet to get the most points.

Violet also had other things to judge.

There was, for example, the Great Zucchini Beauty Contest, in which each girl had dressed a zucchini for a bathing-beauty contest, using anything—cornsilks, hair ribbons, carrot strips, acorn lids.

"Do you see something suspicious about these zucchini?" Vi said to Alicia.

"They all look like Cathy," muttered Alicia. "Even the zucchini aspire to have long blond hair and thin legs."

Vi went out of her way to give the prize to a redheaded zucchini.

The cooks, who were champions at peculiar foods, had had each cabin for an afternoon of candy making. The prizes were, therefore, Sunshine Cabin's One-and-Only Vomit-Green Taffy . . . Ragged Rock Cabin's Own Soggy Marshmallows . . . with of course the real excitement rising over Lakeside Cabin's Personally Puffed Purple Popcorn Balls.

The next event was a horseless horse show.

Charles arranged a circle of clothesline strung on poles, and put four jumps in the ring. Vi was first up. She had to be the horse and jump over all four jumps in her very best form. The campers got to grade her on style, height, and grace.

"Silver ribbon!" called Claudia.

"Why, you scoundrel," said Violet. "I give you my life and you won't give me a blue first place?"

"*And* a poor loser," remarked Claudia. "Next horse up? Cathy."

Cathy simply stared at Claudia. "I'm not doing that."

"All the counselors do it," said Charles. "Come on. Let's see you jump, Cathy."

Cathy was beside herself. She flung her golden hair and stamped her golden foot, looking remarkably like a horse as she did. "I won't make an ass of myself," she hissed at Charles.

"Of course you will," he said impatiently. "That's what the kids love about it. Now get going, Cathy."

Cathy would not budge.

Alicia said very softly, so that the counselor horses could hear, but the campers at the judging stand could not, "Of course, if anybody here does make a good horse's ass, it is Cathy."

The counselors broke down laughing, and Claudia had to wield her whip to bring order among

139

her horses. Marissa went twice, to make up for Cathy not going at all, and they gave her a blue ribbon each time.

Real events—events that require skill—were held after lunch.

There were swimming races and tennis matches, canoe races and archery matches.

By the time the bell was rung for supper, the girls were famished. They staggered into the dining hall, moaning, clutching their empty stomachs, and accusing Charles of starving them. Many threats were made against Charle's life if dinner should be less than perfect.

Even Vi, who dieted every minute, was willing to eat the leaves off the trees. Nevertheless, her cabin was late, and everybody had to wait to say grace until they arrived. Fierce expressions greeted Sunrise Cabin's entrance. Violet sailed past, her girls conspicuous by their freshly applied eye makeup.

Charles, furious, said, "Violet!"

She batted astonishing enormous false eyelashes at him.

Alicia whispered, "They have a stunt planned. Let it go, Charles."

And sure enough, between the clearing of the meal and the serving of dessert, Violet rose to her feet. "Good evening, friends," she began. "And good evening to you also, Charles." She bowed slightly in his direction. "Notice how our clothing is dry and clean, nobody is wearing a bathing suit, and no feet are bare and thus vulnerable to cuts and scrapes."

"I also notice that everybody's face is ready for

a photography session on Madison Avenue," said Charles.

"I have, without doubt, the most stunning campers at Camp Men," said Vi. She knew that Charles hated the nickname Camp Men, as it implied his campers came for an entirely different purpose than the one stated in the camp brochure.

Each dining table seated fourteen. Therefore no table quite fit two whole cabins, so every night the campers rotated down a few seats, and girls sat with different groups as the summer wore on. Violet had gotten her entire cabin at one table. Cathy had been forced to join them.

Vi batted her false eyelashes madly at the entire assemblage of girls.

"My rather spectacularly gifted cabin," began Violet, "has composed a poem."

Many comments surfaced on just how Vi could have reached the conclusion that her cabin was gifted.

"We want everybody to learn our poem, which as you will soon hear, is a passionate and brilliant description of life at Camp Men."

Cathy was a little snide on the subject of learning odes to nature.

Violet's cabin got to their feet. They were all wearing false eyelashes. Very false. As they batted their lengthy black lashes—some of which appeared to be made out of construction paper and held on with Scotch tape—they chanted in perfect unison:

" 'Twas a sweetly Camp Men morning last December in July

141

I brushed a sausage in my hair and put my hairbrush
    on to fry
I swam across the tennis courts and drank a supper
    tray.
The sky lay thick upon the ground while the flagpole
    drove away
Bathing suits were singing sweetly and flip-flops
    bloomed so bright
As the Perch went madly dancing and my sneakers
    took a bite
Happy birthday green zucchini, graduation day is
    past
And I'm a happy camper, diving underground at
    last."

  The girls whistled, clapped, and stomped. "That
is wonderful!" cried Marissa. "I love it. You guys
are so clever."
  Cathy said, "The only thing worse than real poetry is pretend poetry." Nobody paid any attention
to her.

  " 'Twas a sweetly Camp Men morning last December
    in July
I brushed a sausage in my hair and put my hairbrush
    on to fry,"

said Violet. One hundred and fifty girls shouted it
back.

  The reason they were all slow with getting to bed
that night was a very good one. Violet had not been
alone with Marissa long enough to get the details
on her new friendship with Dark. Vi could no longer

stand the suspense, especially when Claudia reported that nobody in Marissa's cabin knew anything, either. "Come on, confess," whispered Vi, walking very slowly. "I'm dying. Take pity on me, Mariss. Didn't I drown for Cathy? Didn't I play horse first? And all for you, Mariss. Friend that I am. Now tell all about Dark. Are you his forever?"

Naturally each of the campers crept along very slowly to hear Marissa's answer. Fear of not finding out slowed everybody down greatly. They even brushed their teeth quietly in the Rain Forest, and tore the toilet paper off quietly in the Perch, lest Marissa should choose that moment to speak. People who normally sounded like elephants storming an African village now walked like dainty weightless gazelles.

And so it was that they tiptoed behind a storage shed that stood between the Rain Forest and the path up the cliff.

And heard—not Marissa's confession—not Violet's pleading—but Brandon and Cathy.

Every foot stopped in midair.

Every breath ceased.

They balanced on each other or gripped handy tree branches.

"You should take up riflery," said Brandon. There was a funny smoochy noise. The girls exchanged knowing glances in the dark.

"I don't approve of guns," Cathy said. "I am totally nonviolent. I would hit a tennis ball but, aim a rifle? Never."

Brandon said, "Cathy. Think."

"I pride myself on my thinking," protested Cathy. "And I think that peace is a very important—"

"Forget peace," said Brandon impatiently. "Think mattress."

The jaws of their hidden audience went slack.

So, presumably, did Cathy's, since she had no answer.

"At the rifle range, you lie down on mattresses in order to shoot," explained Brandon. Or semiexplained. Cathy still had to reach a conclusion. It took the listeners far less time to reach that conclusion than it took Cathy. Every single girl had to jam their hands over their mouths to keep from giggling.

There was no cooing giggle from Cathy. She said solemnly, "Oh. That kind of riflery."

Almost anything might have happened down at the rifle range that night, but regrettably Vi burst out laughing.

Cathy whipped around the shed to see the group of twelve-year-olds with their flashlights all off. And two counselors laughing like hyenas. "You creeps!" screamed Cathy. "You lowlife, spying little—"

She tried to kill them, but joy lent them speed, and after four runs around the shed, Cathy gave up and sat on the steps, crying instead. Brandon, who was definitely on forbidden territory at a forbidden time, slunk away.

Vi's campers fell asleep remarkably fast.

Field day had its uses.

Vi slid out of her sleeping bag and started up the cliff to meet Marissa, but Marissa was already coming down to meet her.

"What a day," whispered Vi. "We whipped Cathy in public time after time. Wasn't it luscious?"

Marissa said nothing.

Vi was anxious. "You aren't still pining after Sin, are you? Now that you have Dark? Cathy is with Brandon anyway."

"Oh, Vi, I don't have Dark! He has so many problems the last thing he wants is a girlfriend. We just sat in the sun listing all the things wrong in our lives. There's a lot more wrong in his life than in mine. His father is going to prison, and I'm going to complain because Sin doesn't want me, because he wants Cathy even if she doesn't want him?"

"I see what you mean."

And, oh—how clearly Violet saw it. Dark was enveloped in his own cloud; that was why the nickname was so good. He and Marissa had met by accident, talked to each other out of misery, and come home together on the motorcycle for convenience.

Vi hugged Marissa. "I know this is dumb," she said. "I admit before I start that it's no substitute. A girl goes to Camp Girl-Meets-Boy, she wants to be met by a terrific boy, that's all."

Around them the soft evening scents of Camp Menunkechogue wafted, and the silvered lake lay smooth beneath a black sky.

"But I got to meet you," said Violet. "We'll be forever friends. And girls last longer than boys and girls. You and I will write forever, and share memories forever. And that's what camp's about."

16

___

"*V*iolet!" shouted Jamie, barreling across the open
fields. Violet's girls were heading in a straggly fashion toward tennis. Violet's cabin was not good at
tennis and welcomed this chance to lag more. "Hi,
Jamie!" they all shouted.

He ran up to Violet without slowing down, without stopping—just picked her up on his way and
whirled her around. Her girls were awestruck. Not
of Jamie—they knew he was strong enough to move
houses—but of Violet. That was the life. Having a
guy swing you around. Her campers sighed happily.

"I get the Jeep tomorrow night," said Jamie. "You
want to go with me into town for the Blueberry
Festival? Can you switch nights with somebody
and get tomorrow night off?"

"Yes," she said, "yes, yes, yes, yes," Violet
hugged him, and Jamie kissed her. Sunrise Cabin
moaned, whistled, stomped, and threw things.

"Have I ever kissed you without a twelve-year-old audience?" said Jamie, kissing her again. "Tonight we'll—"

"Sssshhh," said Violet. "They write to their parents, you know."

"We don't have to," said Claudia eagerly. "We hate writing to our parents. If you let us watch, we'll never write again. Promise."

Jamie said, "You guys run along to tennis now, okay?"

They didn't want to run along until Jamie had kissed Vi again. When would they ever have another opportunity to examine this process so close up? Jamie agreed to kiss her again for educational purposes.

Claudia giggled. "No letters this week, huh, Vi?"

Cathy looked especially lovely that evening. Her Camp Men T-shirt was tied at her waist, exposing her lovely tan, and her shorts were a deep scarlet. In her hair was twisted a matching scarlet rag, as if the camp schedule required relentless hard labor, but she stayed cool and pristine. Everybody else just looked as if they had been sweating. "Little blue fruit?" she said scathingly to Jamie. "Your town holds a celebration for little blue fruit?"

Charles had gathered all the counselors together for another pep talk. They felt pretty peppy even without a talk. Charles just wanted to hear the sound of his own voice again.

"What are you supposed to do?" giggled Cathy. "Go to the church hall and eat shortcake? How can you stand all that excitement?"

"Actually it's not blueberry shortcake, it's blueberry slump," said Jamie cheerfully.

Cathy cooed. "The slump?" She stroked Jamie's Camp Men T-shirt. "That sounds like a laid-back dance."

Jamie immediately began jerking and twisting. At first Marissa thought Cathy had tickled him; then she realized Jamie was dancing. "Suddenly it's nineteen sixty-nine!" shouted Jamie, twitching and leaping. "Vi! Dance the slump with me."

Violet dissolved halfway to the floor. "Slumps," she informed Jamie, "are performed with sagging shoulders."

Before long, they were all slumping. It was obviously a dance that happened down low and required much apelike dangling of arms. Jamie and Violet danced, Cathy and Brandon and Trevor and Sin danced. Marissa leaned on the wall and watched them.

"No, huh?" said Dark to her.

Marissa struggled to smile. "I'm already in a slump," she told him, and Dark laughed. "I know the feeling," he said. He put a comforting brotherly arm around her shoulder and they watched the others let loose.

"So, Jamie, darling," cooed Cathy, "you going to work at a booth? Selling kisses? Selling hot dogs?"

Jamie couldn't imagine why Cathy thought he might be working at a booth.

"Isn't it your little town?" said Cathy. "I thought you were born there or something. Isn't your father like a lumberjack or something?"

While the others shouted with laughter, Jamie heaved a huge proud sigh. Then he beat a tattoo on his chest. "Nope," he said. "My dad's an orthodontist from Queens," Jamie swaggered around the room, proud to be able to pass for a New Englander.

"Are all you boys con artists?" demanded Cathy, irked. "I thought Dark was the only one." She turned slowly, like a model at the end of the runway, spotlights gleaming on her goldenness, and saw Dark with his hand on Marissa's shoulder. Marissa could have told her it was meaningless, but all Cathy saw was that while she had been juggling Trevor, Brandon, and Sin, Violet had actually gotten Jamie, and Marissa had actually gotten Dark.

Cathy's cool voice was like a spray of ice aimed at Dark. "I hear Daddy's gotten an extension, Dark."

It's like standing next to a board, thought Marissa. Dark isn't a person, doesn't have a pulse, he's a yoga master who could end his vital signs at will.

"Adding to his battery of lawyers, isn't he, Dark? Of course, he has the money to do it, huh, Dark?" She exaggerated the nickname, making it silly and stupid.

Violet slumped right into Cathy. The golden-model-at-the-end-of-the-runway image ended when Cathy staggered. But nothing yet had really put Cathy off balance. "Luckily," she cooed, "I have off tomorrow. So you won't be the only one going to that cute little fair, Jamie. Brandon? Trevor? Who wants to take me?"

Violet was beside herself. "Cathy! You promised you'd switch days off with me!" she cried. "I asked you right after tennis. Otherwise I can't go to the fair with Jamie! You promised!"

The beautiful face turned an impenetrable facade on Violet. "How odd. I don't recall."

Violet started to crumple. Her only chance in weeks at a full entire complete perfect day with Jamie and—

"Trade with me, then, Violet," said Marissa. "I won't be going to the fair." When she uttered those words, she thought she had never heard a sentence so sad. There was indeed a summer romance at Camp Girl-Meets-Boy. But it was not Marissa's.

I won't be going to the fair.

"How about a T-shirt?" said Jamie, stopping at a booth which sold everything from sweet little Maine pine tree T-shirts to obscene rock star T-shirts.

He was holding Vi's hand. He had never let go of her hand, actually. Even buying tickets for the Ferris wheel, and paying for the cotton candy (he bought one cone; they ate off opposite sides, and once he licked the sticky sugary threads off Violet's mouth), Jamie never let go of her hand.

Violet was delirious with happiness. The last thing she needed was yet another T-shirt. She felt that once the summer was over, she would never look a T-shirt in the eye again, let alone drape one over her body. And yet—a T-shirt Jamie had bought her?

Heaven in one hundred percent cotton.

"This is a big decision," Violet told him, sqeezing his hand. "It has to be the perfect memento."

Jamie picked a white T-shirt with pine trees spattered on it as if tossed from the end of a paint brush. "Wear it now," he said, paying with one hand.

Violet grinned. "I'll put it on if you promise not to let go my hand," she said.

Violet wriggled into the shirt, using her left hand and Jamie's right hand. There was no way for her to get her right hand into the sleeve unless they traded hands for holding, and Violet refused to. So they walked around the fairgrounds with half the T-shirt on Vi, and the other half wrapped around her like a bandage.

"So you're taking Cathy tonight?" said Marissa to Sin.

They were sitting on the end of the dock, feet dangling in the water, waiting for their campers. Marissa was in short shorts, Sin in jeans. He was right next to her, and the thick seam of his jeans leg was pressed against her bare thigh.

"Cathy doesn't want to go with any one person. A girl like Cathy can't be tied down, you know." Sin actually sounded proud of Cathy for having this feature to her personality.

Why do i still have a crush on this jerk? thought Marissa. Maybe a crush can live with nothing to feed on. Maybe a crush is like a desert cactus: it can get no nourishment at all, and yet it thrives.

It was not a pretty image, and yet how romantic they must look from the shore. Wild clouds and darkening fiery sky must frame their silhouettes for the campers on shore: a girl with rowdy curls, sitting close to a boy with wide, wide shoulders. The girls returning from sports would stare, yearning for the day when they, too, would sit on the end of the dock with a handsome boy.

The dock shuddered under the clatter of feet: Dark bringing the boys for Sin to row back. Sin stood easily and greeted the little boys.

Marissa sat alone.

The boys climbed into the rowboat jabbering and poking each other. It was a difference between girl campers and boy campers: they all talked a mile a minute, but the girls hardly ever had jump-on-your-toes-and-break-them contests. "That everybody?" said Sin, grinning down at his pack of puppies.

Marissa ached to have Sin's smile directed at her.

"You coming with us, Dark?" said Sin.

"No. I've got my canoe. I'll get there first."

All little boys loved a contest. "No, he won't," they yelled. "Sin, you can beat him! Sin, you've got to beat him!"

Dark laughed. "I'll give you a half-lake start, Sin."

Sin put his wonderful shoulders to work, the boys screamed like a work gang, and Dark sat down next to Marissa, putting one arm around her and waving good-bye to Sin with the other. Even though she knew it was a pose for the little boys, to show how utterly relaxed Dark was about winning the "race," Marissa wanted that arm to stay forever.

Her return on the motorcycle that day had come back to haunt her. Her girls were not only sure that Dark would be the perfect Blueberry Festival escort, they were sure that Marissa really was going, even if she had said she wasn't, and would be sneaking out after taps to go with Dark. Once, when he needed a favor, Dark had said, "Please, Mriss," pronouncing her name the way her family did. It had an affectionate sound that "Marissa" by itself didn't. Her girls had all sighed happily. They were content now. Their counselor had a cute boyfriend: they could hold their own in camp gossip.

I wanted my cabin to witness this silhouette, thought Marissa. Or at least Cathy.

Violet had left long ago with Jamie. She had been wearing a lovely, loose prairie skirt in a soft faded blue, with faded lace and a very deep ruffle at the hem. Her blouse was a gathered print, very delicate and full. It all looked inherited from a pioneer great-grandmother. Jamie wore a heavy plaid shirt he probably hoped would make the town mistake him for one of their own.

Marissa didn't know yet what Cathy would wear. But Cathy would parade whatever she chose, and make it clear to Sunset Cabin that Marissa didn't need to dress up, because Marissa wasn't going. "So, Dark," Marissa said wearily, "you going to the festival tonight?"

"Call me Heath, okay? This Dark stuff is beginning to get me down."

"If I call you Heath, Cathy might . . . well—"

He said, "I know. I figure I've got to get used to it. And she'll be an amateur compared to what's waiting at home—from the *Wall Street Journal* to ABC, NBC, and CBS."

"They won't interview you, will they?"

"Nah. It's just when I tune in for the evening news, they'll say in their dead-person voices, *and coming up at eleven, Heath Hester, alleged multimillion-dollar rip-off artist, in the news again.*"

"I see what you mean. I forgot you and your father have the same name."

Heath stood up, flexing his muscles slowly and massaging himself, as if he'd been tied in knots. "I'm actually going to lose the race," he remarked, stepping into his canoe. "Yet another blot on my record."

Very clearly Sin's voice crossed the water. "You're supposed to be canoeing, not flirting, Dark!"

Dark kissed her good-bye.

Marissa was so startled she did not react until Dark was paddling after the rowboat. Had he kissed her because he wanted Sin to think they had been flirting? *Or had he been flirting?*

They had fried ice cream and calzones, they had fried dough and candied apples. They even had blueberry slump. With whipped cream. Violet said, "You realize we are going to have to exchange this medium T-shirt for an extra large if I eat one more calorie."

"Don't talk about dieting," said Jamie. "I hate girls who talk about dieting."

"Some girls have to, though," said Cathy's unmistakable voice.

Violet turned reluctantly.

There stood Cathy, looking absolutely stunning in a white cotton dress that made her the most tan, most golden girl at the entire Blueberry Festival. On her left stood Brandon and on her right, Trevor.

Sin was bringing up the rear. He was carrying Cathy's tote bag. Like some kind of servant.

Cathy laughed at Violet. "You look so cute," she said in her pitying voice. She touched the pine tree T-shirt where Vi had spilled some of the fried ice cream, and where Jamie had spilled some of his blueberry slump.

The pressure of Cathy's eyes was too much. Jamie let go of Vi's hand and Vi took the T-shirt off.

Cathy looked even more amused, as if Vi could never look good enough for Cathy's standards.

"So what shall we do first?" said Cathy. The pleasant ordinary country fair seemed to amuse her even more than Vi's T-shirt.

"We're going to the horse pull," said Jamie. "You can sit with us."

Only Jamie had ever seen a horse pull before: where teams of four or six horses pulled wooden sleds carrying concrete squares. Jamie was entranced by the beauty of the huge sturdy horses. Cathy thought they were ugly. She preferred the delicate-ankled sort of horse she rode back home. Cathy thought it was too dusty, too, the way the horses kicked up the ground. Cathy wanted to go get something to drink.

Violet hoped the boys would say, "Fine, go, we don't care."

And Trevor—who would have guessed that Trevor had character?—did. "I'm gonna watch the pull with Jamie and Violet."

So Sin got Cathy's right side.

Violet thought, For Sin it's Camp Boy-Meets-Girl. He met Cathy. And that's all.

She looked up at Jamie, and he looked down at her. They eyed each other for a moment and then slowly moved toward each other and kissed, a long lingering kiss.

Trevor said, "Could we leave the public entertainment to the horses, please?"

Marissa managed a few precious moments of solitude. She lay on her bunk in Sunset Cabin and daydreamed of Dark—no, Heath—loving her. A real kiss, she asked herself, or a silhouette kiss? If she had known it was coming, she would have paid more attention—maybe picked up a few signals, and so forth.

I want to do it again, thought Marissa. Come on back, Heath, do it again. But it was not Heath who suddenly plopped down on the edge of her bed, making the mattress sag dangerously.

It was Claudia, and Claudia was crying.

Violet had not had as much time alone with Jamie as she would have liked. It occurred to her that, although they had been out several times now, they had never been out alone. Jamie had said something about never kissing her without her campers watching. Well, she thought, you're setting it up like that, fella. Someone's always around to watch.

Vi, Jamie, Cathy, Brandon, Trevor, and Sin rode miniature cars around a hot-rod oval, trying to derail each other. They all got on the Ferris wheel together, and swung their chairs and screamed. They had seconds on blueberry pie and talked about maybe entering the pie-eating contest, but Cathy said they would look stupid, so they didn't.

Violet said, "Jamie?"

"Uh-huh?" Squeezing her hand. Good sign. Vi lowered her voice and dropped back from the others, still arguing pie-eating contest eligibility.

"During the school year," she began slowly, hoping he would interrupt her. "You know?" She played with a hummock of grass by her sneaker. "We don't live all that far away. In real life, I mean."

Suddenly she was holding Jamie's hand, but he was not holding hers. His hand was just lying there.

It was practically a whole different hand. It didn't squeeze or fondle or promise things. Jamie said, "Gee, Vi, school is a long way off. Say, everybody. Look at that. The police constables are getting dunked, in uniform and everything. Come on, let's buy chances and try to dunk cops!"

Two girls on such a narrow cot was tricky, but Marissa had done it a million times. She rolled slightly to give Claudia another inch. Claudia said, "Could you cut my name tape off? It's giving me a blister."

Name tapes, of course, were a bane of camp. At best they were embarrassing—your name scribbled in indelible ink along the waistband of perfectly innocent underpants. But some mothers sewed name tags on. Such tags had a wonderful summer, busily coming off part way, giving blisters to unsuspecting ankles and rashes to the backs of necks. However, it was rarely worth sobs.

Marissa figured it was almost the end of summer and Violet was away for the day and Claudia wanted some attention.

You want attention! thought Marissa. What do you think *I* want? Can't somebody applaud me? Can't somebody comfort me?

She got a grip on herself, found the scissors, and clipped.

"Thanks," said Claudia intensely.

She didn't leave.

Marissa wanted peace and quiet so much she thought she might strangle Claudia. Isn't it enough I have my own eight? she thought. I have to do Violet's campers as well as give up my day off?

"Marissa?" said Claudia in a trembly voice. "Marissa, if you're a really bad person, what should you do?"

Marissa blinked.

Claudia said, "I asked Violet but she just laughed and said I could always throw myself off the cliff. Marissa, it's serious, please be serious with me."

Marissa was touched. She sat up, shoved Claudia lightly to the floor, and began massaging Claudia's shoulders. "Are we talking crimes?" she said. "Lies? Unkindness? What kind of badness?"

Claudia knotted her little fingers in her T-shirt. What a bony little thing she was: thin and preadolescent, without the slightest hint of the teenager she would be next year. "You know how Violet says that clothing is life and life is clothing and how we all laugh at her?"

"Yes."

Claudia gulped. "I actually feel that way," she whispered. "I'm actually glad my mother chose that plum gown with the ivory lace because I want to wear it. I've been writing them hate letters, but I'm so excited about being in two weddings I can hardly stand it. Oh, Marissa, *I'm glad they got divorced, because I get to wear such great dresses this fall!*"

Claudia began sobbing terrible, desperate shoulder-wracking sobs. Marissa hauled her back up on the bed and rocked her. "You found a silver lining, Claudia. And that's okay. Out of all this mess, you get one bonus. Terrific clothes. Don't worry. You aren't bad. You're just going to have a bigger wardrobe."

They lay on their backs together. Claudia talked,

and Marissa studied the ceiling boards, and the crack where mice ran in and out.

I'm older and wiser, thought Marissa. Vi had fun all summer, but I grew up. *And Claudia knew*. It shows.

"Square dancing!" cried Cathy. "Oh, how cute! Let's square dance."

The boys moaned. They didn't know how to square dance. They could never learn how to square dance. They didn't like square dancing. Square dancing made them ill.

"Nonsense!" cried Cathy. "The caller tells you what to do, and it's very easy. You just get thrown from partner to partner and have a lovely lovely time."

"She's right," said the fiddle player. "Come on, guys, do what the lady says. We need men. Get in there, make fools of yourselves."

Cathy flounced her skirts prettily, and took each boy by the hand, arranging them in a square even as they said "No." "No." "Cathy, *I won't*." "No!"

Violet thought, She'll look beautiful, and I'll look stupid. She'll dance with Jamie, too. Jamie's not holding my hand anymore and Cathy's gloating.

What had been wrong about suggesting they might date during the school year? Did Jamie have a girlfriend back home? Did Jamie think Vi was only good enough for July and August?

"I don't want to square dance," Vi mumbled.

"Oh, come on," said Cathy. "You'll be cute, Vi, don't worry so much about being clumsy."

And then a wonderful thing happened.

Justice.

Full squares of eight weren't forming neatly. There were too many girls in some and too many beginners in others. So the fiddler put Brandon over with two thrilled thirteen-year-old girls, and put Trevor over with a laughing matron his mother's age, and Sin with a tall slim girl in her twenties, wearing a blueberry-stained apron. The blueberry girl kissed Sin upon introduction, and her blueberry stained lips left a blue stain on his.

And Cathy, golden and white Cathy, was partnered with a man whose beer belly was too large to be covered by his dirty shirt. And also in Cathy's square were a weedy old man, and his two giggly grandchildren, and a thick, stolid, unsmiling couple who looked ready to apply for divorce.

Cathy was almost crying.

Vi yelled, "You look cute, Cathy. Don't worry so much about being clumsy."

17

Camp was shooting toward the end of summer faster than a canoe across the lake.

Violet felt that she was being hurtled across time—she had never bargained on giving up so easily. She no sooner woke up to Janey's reveille than she was collapsing to taps. The campers who had been there all summer went through a fourth-session slump: they felt they had done all, seen all, hiked all. And then, without anybody grasping that it was so close, fifth and final session began, and with it the knowledge that summer was ending.

How could the long hot dusty days be wrapping up?

And yet they were.

Nights are chillier, Violet thought.

(The cabin doing weather reports said no.)

But one cool night, the girls sat on the edge of the dock, shivering in their long-sleeved, hooded Camp Men sweatjackets, and Laury whispered, "Look. Look at that tree! It's half autumn."

161

And far across the lake, beyond the boys' camp, where the trees went solidly to the edge of the water, as if planning a bridge, autumn was coming. Patches of bright colors pierced the green leaves. The trees were bragging to each other like campers: *I'm* redder than *you* are.

And that night the sun set fiercely, as if raging against the end of summer. Hot orange and purple streaks savaged the sky, and torn clouds chased themselves. Wind ruffled the waters of the lake. There was no mirrorlike reflection of that vivid sky: just volcanic color on the waves.

Silently, the girls watched the sun set. At the beginning of summer they would not have slowed down long enough to glance across the lake, nor cared to. Now they were absorbed by the sunset, perhaps even awed.

And in each heart beat an age-old cry: *summer ended so fast!*

"Do you know what a summer romance is?" said Violet.

"No," said Marissa glumly. She dangled her toes in the cold lake water.

"It's a timed event on the field day of Earth," said Violet.

Every camper repeated this softly to herself. Even Cathy repeated it.

"A race to the finish," cried Violet. "Speed counts . . . but not necessarily style."

Marissa thought this was horrifying. She would have to think about it for a while. Of course, she had a lot more time to herself for thinking than Violet did. If Violet had a spare moment, Jamie absorbed it. But—but if so—why was Violet saying that a summer romance was a timed event? Was time running out on Violet? Was Jamie a thing that would end when camp did?

"Speak for yourself, Vi," said Cathy cruelly. "I feature both speed and style."

The next morning was the third to the last day, and the campers began to prepare their ghost rocks for the last campfire. Everybody found a smooth rock that sat comfortably in her hand. In crafts, the girls took the waterproof paints in ten colors, and each girl painted her rock with two coats of base. Claudia had chosen lime green, but almost everybody else exhibited a little taste and went for red or blue.

The second to the last day they painted their messages on the rocks.

Claudia wrote, *"No more Perching!"*

"Is that how you want future generations of campers to remember you, Claudia?" demanded Vi. "The girl on the Perch?"

There was quite a selection of messages for the future.

Free at Last.

I love Camp Men.

I think lice are rather nice.

Alicia went berserk. "There are not now and there never have been lice at this camp!" she shrieked.

"But it rhymes," said Janey, hurt.

The camp musical was that night, and afterward, campfire.

They had huggles. Huggles were a cross between hugging and snuggling. You had to think up a specially nice thought, write it down, and put your thought inside a brown paper bag with teddy bears

163

drawn on it. Then you put the bag on the campfire, and the huggles burned up.

"That is sick," Violet said to Charles. "Burning your good thoughts? That is twisted, Charles."

Charles said that now the good thoughts were wafting on the smoke, through the air, and going into your lungs.

"That sounds more like cancer," objected Claudia.

"You people have a terrible attitude!" cried Charles.

But he was wrong. Their huggles had been carefully decided. Laury did not know whether her huggle should be for Violet, who aired her mattress so often without saying anything, or for Dark, who gave her the watch alarm that helped her to get up. In the end Laury decided on a double huggle. *May Violet and Dark find as much happiness as they gave me*, she wrote, and quickly folded her huggle, stuffed it in the bag, and threw the bag on the fire.

May Marissa be right, wrote Claudia, *let me not be a bad person for wanting to be in two weddings.*

Dana wrote, *Thank you God for Camp Men.*

Janey, who had gotten to know Dark pretty well what with all her trumpet lessons, wrote, *Take care of Dark when he gets home, God, and don't let him cry.* Janey was crying when she wrote it.

Final sports events were held on the last full day. This time, most events were water sports: canoes, and swimming, and diving, and water polo, and water tag, and water relays. Vi was on shore, checking people off, making sure everybody had a buddy. She had a clipboard (Vi loved clipboards; you felt so official) and everybody else had a towel.

There was laughter and shouting, splashing and silliness, but a strange heaviness lay over everything, like an invisible fog. Even though camp speed-records were set twice, the day and the campers seemed to move slowly. They tried to enfold every moment in memory, for they were not just racing to the finish line—they were, as Vi had told them, racing away from Camp Menunkechogue.

Charles never changed or bent rules, so even on this last day—perhaps especially on this last full day—they had rest hour. The campers went to their bunks more easily than normal, but few slept. They mostly lay on their backs and stared at the ceilings. Vi's cabin had finished the entire ceiling: miniature boxes of Froot Loops, Cheerios, Rice Krispies, and Cocoa Puffs totally covered the inside. Charles had not looked up all summer, and the boxes would stay all winter, and be there—probably rather moldy for wear—when the new Sunrise Cabin took residence next June twentieth.

Some of the counselors played Ping-Pong during rest hour.

The last rest hour, thought Marissa.

Jamie tapped a ball gently toward Vi. If the Ping-Pong ball had been round, it would have reached her, but all the camp balls were semicrushed, and it veered off to the right. Violet missed.

"My paddle doesn't even have any rubber on it," Vi complained.

"Adds to the excitement," said Jamie.

Cathy raised her lovely eyebrows. "Excitement? In Ping-Pong?"

Sin said, "Want to play me, Cathy?"

"No," said Cathy.

And even then, Sin looked after her with yearning. Marissa wanted to kick him in the shins. Was this to be her memory of Sin—the memory she would carry home with her faded T-shirts and ripped sneakers—Sin a little whipped puppy crawling behind Cathy?

Vi quit. Cathy took her place. Jamie grinned and played killer Ping-Pong.

Heath and Marissa and Vi went outside to sit in the shade, and stare at the lake. Nobody could think of anything to say. You felt as if on the last night you should say only meaningful things, or very witty things, but you could not be ordinary.

"You have such crazy girls, Vi," said Heath. "Janey and Claudia and Dana and Laury. What's it been like to live with them full time?"

Vi giggled. "Like I'm the keeper in a small zoo. Cleaning up after little animals other keepers wouldn't keep."

They all laughed, and unexpectedly, Heath hugged both the girls. He pulled Marissa in on his left and Vi in on his right. "I just want to say, before this ends," he said, "that you two have gotten me through the summer."

"*We* have?"

"You're nice. And funny. And good company. And I'll miss you."

They were crying then, and hugging him and both wiping their eyes on his T-shirt.

"It'll never come back," cried Marissa. "This summer is gone forever, and all we'll have is little patches of memory."

166

"But good little patches," said Vi. "And we'll be back next year, won't we?"

But nobody knew whether they would be back next year. It was scary. Where was next year? What was it? With whom?

The gong rang.

Everybody straggled down to the girls' campfire. It was so odd to be sharing the hotdog roast with the boys—the only time they had shared a meal like that. It made things even more strange, because they didn't really know what to say to each other, or where to sit, or even how to sit. They just milled around, putting ketchup and mustard on everything, sorry this very last night was different from all the precious nights before.

Even the S'mores were spoiled.

The boys had different S'mores jokes than the girls, and although it was fun to slurp in your melted marshmallow and have it dripping on your chin when there were just girls around, it was embarrassing in front of the boys.

Nothing ruins a S'mores faster than having to be neat.

After S'mores came counselor stunts and spoofs. And when the campers finished clapping, they saw that the sun had set. Charles sent the boys to their canoes, and they went quietly: the canoes black against a black lake, the paddles splashing softly, intimately, in the dark.

On Vi's cheek tears splashed, and Laury's hand not Jamie's, took hers, and Vi thought, It's over. He paddled away. It was my summer romance, my camp romance. I won't marry him the way Gretchen married Michael.

167

"Final campfire," said Marissa softly, and they all turned away from the black mirror lake and the vanishing boys.

A hundred and fifty girls sat on the cool damp sand and grass, and the sounds of night drifted through the thick trees. Some girls were already crying, because in the morning, parents would come; camp would be over forever and ever. Everybody laid one dry twig for the kindling.

Charles lit the final campfire.

And then one by one, as they swayed together, arms around each other, singing the camp songs, each girl got up and put her ghost stone down, starting a new fire circle. It would end their summer, but next year, it would be the fire circle: the one the new girls would sit around.

Laury and Dana went up. Claudia and MarMar. Roxanne and Janey. JoAnne, Esther, and Meg. Each little ghost stone was piled on the others, their painted colors hardly visible in the dark, their words flickering by the firelight.

I love Marissa.
I learned reveille at last!
Dana was here.
Don't forget me!
Best bunkmate on earth.

Violet tried not to cry. Not one girl in her cabin had dedicated a ghost stone to her. All summer she had loved and cherished these crazy idiots. Did they not remember their first facials on the mountain? The ice-cream pizza? The Green-Eyed Maniac?

Ghost stones were over.

Charles led them in the pledge.

And then all the campers from Sunrise Cabin stood up, producing a huge and hideously lime-green stone. "We don't want this stone to become a ghost," said Claudia. "We want it to last as long as Camp Menunkechogue does." The girls staggered forward, dropping the huge neon-green rock awkwardly near all the littler, saner rocks.

We love Vi.

Violet sat with the tears running down her cheeks, mopping them up with her sweatshirt sleeve, and when her girls came back to the circle, she tried to take all of them in her lap. "I'll miss you so much!"

And she knew when she did have children some day, she wouldn't care if they were crazy like Claudia, or bed wetters like Laury, or pesky like Dana. She would just love them. With all her heart.

They sang every verse of all the old songs, the ones everybody had refused to learn the first night because they were so dumb.

"We have to have a reunion!" cried Marissa.

They huggled for real. Everybody took a jillion photographs and cried some more. And Charles gave a special closing speech. It was short, the way all good speeches are short.

But it had a surprise ending.

Camp does not often have surprises. Especially Camp Menunkechogue, where Charles took pride in doing everything exactly as it had been done when he was a boy. And so nobody even once thought that Charles might have a surprise on the last night.

"My friends," he said softly, "campers and counselors, cooks and crew. In the midst of all the hikes and mosquito bites, the lumpy mattresses and the lovely sunsets, the laughter and the praise, there has been a romance going on."

Waves lapped softly on the shore.

A loon cried hauntingly.

Trees creaked in the wind above their heads.

"Alicia and I," said Charles, full of pride, "are getting married."

18

"Why didn't you *tell* us?" demanded Vi.

"Why didn't we *see*?" moaned Marissa.

"The nurse and the manager," said Violet disapprovingly. "That doesn't have a very romantic ring, Alicia. You should have better titles."

Alicia had not stopped smiling since campfire. "I will have the title of part owner of Camp Menunkechogue, how does that sound? And ours will be the first wedding of Camp Men leaders."

"Will not," cried Vi. "My cousin Gretchen married Michael, and they were both—"

Alicia screamed. "Gretchen is your cousin? But I love Gretchen! I was Gretchen's counselor! Ooooh, Vi, why didn't you tell me the first minute we met?"

Station wagons parked on the grass.

Foot lockers tumbled down the steep paths, dragging their owners after them.

* * *

"I'm going, Vi," whispered Dana.

•Dana's parents thanked Vi for teaching Dana that camp could be fun. Dana's brother thanked Vi for keeping Dana half the summer and asked next year, could Vi keep her all summer please?

"I'll miss you, Dana," whispered Vi.

She waved the whole time they were driving across the fields, until they were lost to sight.

Car horns tooted au revoir.
Addresses were scribbled on the backs of old envelopes.

"I thought you were jealous of Cathy, though," said Vi.

Alicia had never looked so totally like Mary Poppins: smug and neat and china doll. "I was, of course. Charles flirted right back with her, and made exceptions for her. I seriously considered her early death in a painful manner. But in the end, it worked out nicely. Because it gave me a chance to say, 'Okay, Charles, make up your mind. Are we engaged or not?' "

"Ooooooooh," moaned Vi, so caught up in the secret romance she almost forgot her feud with Charles. "What if he had said 'not?' "

Alicia's smile was smug. It said, I knew perfectly well what Charles would say. He would say, Alicia, please marry me.

Best friends struck final poses.
Photographs were taken, Polaroids exchanged.

* * *

172

"I'm going, Vi," said Claudia.

Vi gave her a hug they both thought would never stop. "Now, you look beautiful at those weddings," she ordered Claudia.

"I will."

"You catch those bouquets, and toss one to me, now, you hear?" said Vi.

Claudia giggled. "You're not invited."

"What? I forced you to write to your mother and Jonathan, your father and Heather Anne—and those thankless people are not inviting me to their weddings? Disgraceful."

They had to joke.

Or cry.

"Good-bye, Claudia," whispered Vi, and it was a whisper because her throat tightened, and nothing more came out.

Claudia started for her car, and then came back, only to hurtle into Marissa's arms this time. "Mriss?" Crying.

" 'Bye, honey." Crying also.

"Thank you. For—well—you know." A fierce hug, a second one for Vi, and flight to the car, so it would all be over with.

Marissa and Violet waved even after Claudia's car had vanished into the Maine woods.

"When's the wedding?" said Marissa, wiping away her tears.

"What will your dress be like?" said Vi. Vi hoped the dress was going to be wonderful because the groom certainly wasn't.

"I haven't thought about dates or dresses yet," said Alicia.

Violet told Alicia she was weird.

Alicia said severely, "You should not get so. excited by the frills of a ceremony, Violet. Love, loyalty, honor, and kindness matter more."

Violet looked doubtful. All that for Charles?

She loved to think about *her* wedding. She had been reading brides' magazines long before Gretchen married Michael. She liked to plan her honeymoon and her first house and her first budget and her first meals.

She wondered if Jamie was her true love. Or just one in a line of loves to come? Which would be nicer, really? Jamie forever? Or Jamie lost in the mists of a dozen memorable charmers?

A magnificent Jaguar pulled up. There was something incredibly sexy about its restrained colors and sleek power. They were sure it had to be Dark's father: they were about to see the criminal of the year in the flesh. But a young man got out. He moved very slowly, as if advertising himself. Cathy ran up to him.

Brandon, Trevor, and Sin stared.

There was a long, deep, intimate embrace, well rehearsed.

"I'd like you to meet some of the friends I made here," said Cathy, tugging the young man into the crowd of counselors. Of all people, she started introductions with Vi.

"Not friends exactly," muttered Violet.

But the young man misunderstood. He thought Violet meant these boy counselors were more than friends. He said sharply to Cathy, "You dated these guys?"

"Of course I didn't, Channing, darling, I'm totally faithful to you always."

Cathy winked at the boys, and sashayed out of their lives, into the Jaguar, down the rutted road.

Trevor and Brandon managed to laugh.

Sin did not.

Three hundred children and their parents leaving in two hours? They were dizzy with good-byes, worn out with tears.

Campers stuck a last toe in the beloved lake.

Promises to return were tossed like pebbles in the water.

"Sin?" said Marissa. "You okay?"

"No. I'm a jerk. I was a jerk all summer. Do you know how it feels to look back at ten whole weeks and know you were a jerk twenty-four hours a day, seven days a week, adding up to a total jerkhood of one thousand six hundred and eighty hours?"

They were laughing then, slowly at first, and with mounting hysteria, while Sin imitated himself with Cathy. "Marissa, why didn't you just shoot me?"

Marissa was doing a little arithmetic. "Actually, Sin, she wasn't here the first two weeks. You can subtract three hundred thirty-six hours of jerkhood. Now, don't you feel better?"

"Congratulations, Charles," said Violet. Charles did not look romantic to her. He looked like a pain-

175

in-the-neck camp manager with bad posture. But Alicia loved him and Violet loved love.

Charles said, "I owe you an apology, Vi."

"Or ten," agreed Vi.

"For trying to make Janey quit blowing reveille. I had my priorities wrong. You were correct."

Vi accepted the first apology graciously. "And?"

"And what?"

"And what about the ethnic slurs on my makeup, and the unfair treatment of us compared to Cathy, and yelling at me because my horror stories are so excellent that screaming naturally—"

"Makeup is not ethnic," said Charles.

Violet sniffed. "I have to kiss a camper good-bye. We will continue our fight next summer, Charles." She was a foot shorter than he was, but she was tall as she stalked off. Charles slumped.

"Next summer?" he muttered to Alicia. "That ding-a-ling mascara tube thinks I'd hire her again?"

"And she's right, of course," said Alicia, snuggling.

Jamie's orthodontist father was coming for him.

Introduce me, please? thought Vi. Then I'll know you want to brag about me. I'll know there's a chance we'll date this year. " 'Bye, Jamie," was all she managed.

Jamie took her hand. "Let's walk around," he muttered, "I'm a nervous wreck." They walked toward the water. The new campfire circle, its red and blue and yellow ghost stones garish by day, lay between them and the lake. Jamie read the huge lime-green one out loud. "We love Vi," he said softly.

Vi shrugged. "Nice rock, huh?"

He circled the fire circle, reading the others. "The best one, Vi."

Violet pressed her teeth together. "I'll miss you, Jamie." *Tell me I don't need to because we'll be going out!*

Jamie held her in his arms.

"I had a wonderful summer," he said. "You're a wonderful girl."

Violet had never heard a closing line to a romance before, but she was pretty sure this was it.

"Jamie!" yelled Charles. "Your dad is here!"

And it was done; he was gone. Violet thought, I wanted to come to Camp Girl-Meets-Boy, and I came, and I conquered every fear, and made friends with every camper, and I had a wonderful boyfriend. And maybe he will call. I'm going to pretend he's going to call.

She waved good-bye, and Jamie blew her a kiss, and Vi hung onto that: that kiss, like milkweed caught in midair.

Dark came up behind Marissa. She had just blown a kiss to two of her girls and she was wiping away tears.

"I'll miss you," said Dark.

They hugged, an intense hug, as if there really had been a lot between them during the summer. Marissa began crying again.

"Not every summer can be a best summer," Dark told her.

"Next summer? Do you think it will be best?"

He shrugged, "That's the thing about next summer. You can hope. I don't know of two nicer words than *next summer*."

The Jeep pulled up next to them. Charles said, "Okay, Heath. Let's see, I'm taking you, and Brandon, and Violet to the airport, right? Let's get going. And Sin, you're driving Marissa to the bus station, and Marissa, you have the ticket to get to your aunt's in Boston, right?"

Marissa nodded.

Heath said very softly, "Mriss? Maybe we could get together after school starts."

Her heart leaped so hard she thought he could probably feel it through his shirt. She said, "That would be lovely." She thought, Is that all I can say? Heath wants to see me again, and all I can come up with is a dignified, boring thing like *that would be lovely*?

Heath touched her hair lightly.

"If I don't see you," said Marissa, "be strong, Heath. I'll be thinking about you." She managed a trembly smile. "I put a huggle for you in my brown paper bag. So did Janey, you know. And Laury."

Heath put on his sunglasses quickly and got in the Jeep. She would never know if he was starting to hide again—or hiding tears.

Marissa and Violet did not know how to say goodbye.

"Write me?" Lumps in the throat like balls of pain.

"Of course I will. Phone me?" A voice that shook.

"Of course I will." Swallows that wouldn't go down.

"Tell me what happens between you and—you know."

178

"Of course I will."

"Forever friends?" As if it could be otherwise.

"Forever friends." A promise.

" 'Bye."

" 'Bye!

Just a whisper, a wish on the wind that it didn't have to be.

And then waves through the Jeep window, nothing left of two best friends but a hand in the distance.

Sin had Alicia's old Chrysler to take Marissa to the corner where the bus stopped: rural Maine didn't exactly have stations. They tossed Marissa's duffel in, and her plastic bag of arts and crafts gifts from the girls, her plastic bag of laundry, and her plastic bag of her own treasures. She was still a little-girl camper: she still stooped to pick up the perfect acorn lid, the finest baby pinecone, the softest feather.

"It ended so fast I couldn't get a grip on it," she told Sin. "All of a sudden the people I spent my summer with were shooting out of here like stars."

He nodded. "I know. When I said good-bye to my campers, nobody knew what to do. We wanted to hug and kiss but ten-year-old boys want to be grown-ups and they never hug and kiss."

Marissa laughed. "I think the more grown up you get, the *more* you want to hug and kiss."

"Tell that to a ten-year-old boy."

She wanted to tell it to Sin, but she didn't. Do I still want Sin to hug and kiss me, she wondered, or is it Dark I want now? And is it Dark I want—

mysterious unknown stranger—or Heath, boy in pain?

They got in Alicia's car, and drove away.

"Stop the car a second, Sin."

"Why? Forget something?"

"Just because."

Sin stopped.

Marissa let camp soak into her. She looked at the steep hill on the west, covered with thick green firs, its paths to the cabins hidden, only the little white, pointing-finger signs visible at the bottom. She looked at the wide grassy meadow, where they had played volleyball, and badminton, and softball, and had parades, and tournaments. She looked over at the common room. It would need a fresh coat of white paint for next year. The screens would have to be replaced in the dining room, but the dock still gleamed, and the bobbling markers around the crib were still scarlet. The sun glittered on the lake, and the lake was quiet, waiting for next year.

No T-shirts were draped on the bushes to dry.

No navy blue tank suits dove off the dock.

No art projects were on display in the common room.

No kids at supper were on the fourteenth verse of a naughty camp song.

"You're so romantic," said Sin. "It's just camp, okay?"

But it wasn't just camp.

For Marissa it would never be "just" anything.

* * *

Hundreds of cars from dozens of camps headed south, leaving the woods, leaving Maine, going home.

And in every heart, beat the magic words:

Next summer.

Read about life after camp when Violet and Marissa and their friends are reunited in CAMP REUNION!

ABOUT THE AUTHOR

Caroline B. Cooney is the award-winning author of several novels for young adults, including *The Face on the Milk Carton, Family Reunion, Among Friends, The Girl Who Invented Romance, I'm Not Your Other Half* and *Don't Blame the Music*. She lives in Westbrook, Connecticut.

STARFIRE

Romance Has Never Been So Much Fun!

☐ **IN SUMMER LIGHT**
By Zibby Oneal   25940-7 $3.50
The last place on earth Kate wants to spend the summer
is at home with her parents. Kate can't escape the
overpowering presence of her father, a famous artist who
insists on ruling everybody's life, including her own.
Then graduate student Ian Jackson arrives, and much to
Kate's surprise the handsome young man helps Kate
learn about herself and see her father in a new light.

☐ **CAMP GIRL-MEETS-BOY**
By Caroline B. Cooney   27273-X $3.50
Welcome to Camp Menunkechogue! For Marissa, finally
a counselor, camp is what she lives for. For Vi, camp is a
place to meet and catch a boyfriend. Grab your gear and
join them for camp songs, romance, and great summer
friendships!

☐ **CAMP REUNION**
By Caroline B. Cooney   27551-8 $3.50
Everyone's invited to Camp Men for a weekend reunion.
Tans have faded but not the memories as Vi and Marissa
meet up with their summer loves. Will it work out this
time around?

STARFIRE

Books *you'll* want to read...and keep

☐ **HOME SWEET HOME**
by Jeanne Betancourt
16-year-old Tracy Jensen is not looking forward to leaving New York City to move with her family to her grandmother's farm. Tracy feels isolated at first, but when she meets Russian exchange student Anya and gets involved in the town's activities she sees that life on the land offers many more rewards than she'd ever anticipated. 27857-6 $2.95/$3.50 in Canada

☐ **THE SILVER GLOVE**
by Suzie McKee Charnas
Heroine of *The Bronze King*, 14-year-old Valentine Marsh must help her remarkable, magical grandmother fight a powerful wizard who's come to Earth to steal human souls—and is masquerading as Val's new school psychologist! *The Silver Glove* is full of suspense, chilling chase scenes, magic & love. 27853-3 $2.95/$3.50 in Canada

□ CAUGHT IN THE ACT: ORPHAN TRAIN
QUARTET, BOOK 2 by Joan Lowery Nixon
In the second novel of THE ORPHAN TRAIN
QUARTET, 11-year-old, Mike fears that he will be sent
back to New York City to serve his prison sentence as
a convicted thief. But the German family which has
adopted him seems to be involved in much worse than
stealing—murder! Mike vows to uncover the truth,
even if his own life is in danger.
27912-2 $2.95/$3.50 in Canada

□ THE GIRL WHO INVENTED ROMANCE
by Caroline B. Cooney, author of 'Among Friends'
As she watches her friends and family playing at
romance, 16-year-old Kelly Williams has a great idea—
she'll create a board game that sets down the rules of
the romance game. It's easy for Kelly to see how others
should act, but it's much more difficult when it comes to
her own feelings for Will! (A Starfire Hardcover).
05473-2 $13.95/$15.95 in Canada